HIDE AND SEEK

Bishop turned to the window and flashed his rejoinder: "Who's there?"

A moment later, he received the reply: "Oz."

Bishop responded: "Oz who?"

Satisfied it was Bishop, the American chopper crew sent: "What's your situation?"

Bishop replied hastily: "Hidden inside washroom. Rebels searching. Will soon be found."

"Should we attempt rescue?"

"Yes. Let us know when. Will create a diversion."

A dark cloud briefly covered the sun; when it had cleared, a final message flashed from the chopper: "Will return ASAP."

HarperPaperbacks by
Duncan Long

NIGHT STALKERS
GRIM REAPER
TWILIGHT JUSTICE
DESERT WIND
SEA WOLF

DUNCAN LONG *Night* STALKERS
SHINING PATH

HarperPaperbacks
A Division of HarperCollins*Publishers*

This is a work of fiction. The characters, incidents, and
dialogues are products of the author's imagination and
are not to be construed as real. Any resemblance to actual
events or persons, living or dead, is entirely coincidental.

HarperPaperbacks *A Division of* HarperCollins*Publishers*
10 East 53rd Street, New York, N.Y. 10022

Cover art by Edwin Herder

First printing: May 1991

Printed in the United States of America

HarperPaperbacks and colophon are trademarks of
HarperCollins*Publishers*

10 9 8 7 6 5 4 3 2 1

PROLOGUE

Harlan Lloyd thumbed the safety of his Calico M100 carbine, a shiver sweeping over his lanky frame as he crouched in the cool darkness of the Andean night. The red-haired geologist scrutinized the surroundings for the intruders the sentry had warned were approaching, swiftly checking the others hiding in the trench beside him behind the stone barricade.

Satisfied they were secure for the moment, the American glanced down at the woman kneeling next to him, her thin face and ebony hair half-lit by moonlight, reminding him of an ancient Incan goddess. As her copper bracelets clanked softly against the bullpup stock of her rifle, she looked up at him.

"When will they come?" she asked in heavily accented Spanish that bore traces of Aymara—the language of most of the villagers.

"Anybody's guess," the geologist shrugged, replying in English. Noting her puzzled expression, he shifted to Spanish. "The lookout said they were a mile away, so they should be here soon," he explained. *If this isn't another false alarm,* he added to himself.

Maria reached over to give his arm a squeeze,

then returned her attention to the trail that led toward them. Lloyd tugged his heavy poncho around himself, shifting his weight to get his knee off a sharp pebble that was digging into his flesh. Suddenly, the villager crouched to his left nudged him. "There, by the brush," the man whispered, pointing. "Someone is coming up the path."

The geologist smiled grimly to himself. Perhaps the time he'd spent in the U.S. Marines was finally paying off after all.

The guerrillas were now climbing the trail that had been altered to appear the most convenient for them. *And in doing so,* Lloyd thought to himself, *they're slipping right into our killing zone—IF the villagers will wait for the order to fire.* "Remember," the geologist whispered to the men and women on either side of him, "hold your fire until I give the order. Pass the word along our lines."

Armed only with the .22 rifles and shotguns the Peruvian government permitted the villagers to own, it was essential the guerrillas come to within a hundred meters of them. Otherwise, the ineffectual .22 bullets and low-velocity shotgun pellets would fail to kill; the guerrillas would only retreat to within several hundred yards of the village and pick off the natives with their more powerful machine guns and military rifles.

The American geologist turned to the black-cloaked figure crouched behind him. "Father Ramero, are you ready?" he asked.

The priest's even teeth reflected the moonlight, the only sign that the swarthy-skinned man was there, waiting in the darkness. "Ready," he answered quietly, stroking the blasting machine's scarred, wooden handle that stood like a crucifix in the shadows.

Lloyd squinted down the trail that wound toward the village, trying to discern the enemy's number.

Fifteen? No, more like twenty, perhaps twenty-five, were slowly climbing the incline into the trap. And they're bunched up, he noted.

A good sign.

It meant they were poorly trained and suspected nothing; otherwise they'd be spread out. With luck, they'd pay dearly for the terror they'd unleashed among his adopted people.

The American held his breath as the point man of the Shining Path squad neared the killing zone. "Come on," the geologist urged the intruder under his breath. "Don't stop now, you stupid *bastardo.*"

The insurgent neared the booby trap buried in the trail and stepped on the first of four crude traps each consisting of a shotgun cartridge jammed inside a bit of rusty pipe mounted to a plank of wood. The weight of the guerrilla's foot shoved the cartridge downward against a nail that acted like a firing pin; the shell immediately discharged, ripping off the front of the man's foot in a savage blast that lit the night for a moment and echoed from the bluff above the village.

Lloyd whirled to face the priest. "Now!" he shouted, forgetting in his excitement to speak Spanish.

Even if he hadn't understood English, the priest would have understood the command. He gripped the plunger of the blasting machine and shoved it downward with a practiced, steady stroke. The generator inside the box sent an electrical current through the wires leading from the wall behind which the villagers were hidden.

The current sizzled at the speed of light through the snaking wires to the blasting caps and sticks of dynamite planted along the trail. The deafening explosion hurled a deadly fusillade of rusty nails, glass, and rocks at the unsuspecting guerrillas; those standing closest to the blast were slashed to ribbons by the shrapnel, lifeless before their shattered bodies even fell to the earth.

Five of the wounded guerrillas remained standing, lifting their rifles to fire at their unseen attackers.

"Tirar!" Lloyd yelled, ordering the villagers to fire.

The line of native Peruvians vaulted to their feet, releasing an angry hail of bullets and shotgun pellets.

The guerrillas, caught in the deadly salvo, dropped to the ground, one lone AKM blazing in the night until its magazine was exhausted, its dead owner's finger locked in the trigger guard.

The forms lay still on the blood-stained hillside.

"Dejar de tirar," Lloyd yelled. "Cease fire."

His order was reiterated by the villagers closest to him and abruptly the shooting stopped. For three seconds all was peaceful, then a rasping moan floated up to them from the trail below.

"Get down," Lloyd ordered his comrades. The Shining Path fighters were devious, the geologist knew, perfectly capable of faking death or injury to lure the naive villagers.

But someone would have to go and ascertain that the guerrillas were either dead or harmless. He didn't give himself time to brood on it but straightened his

6′8″-frame and freed himself from Maria's grip on his arm.

"Stay here," he ordered the villager who stepped forward to accompany him. "I'm going alone."

The American crept catlike down the path toward the fallen guerrillas lying motionless under the bright full moon.

Most of the insurgents were obviously dead—two were barely recognizable as having been human beings, but the one who moaned was obviously very much alive.

Lloyd approached the man from behind, crossing a low boulder to give the remaining booby traps on the path a wide berth. From his vantage point he studied the huddled form rocking back and forth in the moonlight, clutching at the stump of an arm.

The American geologist climbed down from the boulder and approached the guerilla, lifting his M100 to cover the wounded man. He was unsure what to do, realizing how naive it had been to assume all of the fighters would either be killed outright or would try to resist capture and have to be eliminated.

There were no plans for dealing with an injured prisoner.

The unarmed rebel sat on his haunches, staring with wide eyes at the American giant towering over him. *"Misericordia!"* the guerrilla pleaded, his voice quivering in pain.

Centering his gun's glow-in-the-dark sight on the man's forehead, Lloyd fought to swallow as his finger tightened on the trigger of the .22 rifle loaded with hollow-point, hyper-velocity bullets.

Three seconds ticked away as the guerrilla and

the American stared at each other. Finally, the geologist's breath erupted from his lungs as he released the trigger, lowering the rifle with shaky hands.

The rebel doubled over and wept, still holding the stump of his arm. Then he resumed rocking back and forth, sobbing in a low, guttural voice.

A dark figure swam into the edge of Lloyd's vision.

The geologist whirled around, raising his rifle.

"It's only me," Father Ramero cautioned, his teeth glinting in the moonlight.

The geologist was silent, knowing it would do no good to warn the priest to be more careful. *God, it's a miracle I didn't shoot him,* he thought. Then he turned his attention back to the weeping guerilla. "I don't know what we should do with him, Father Ramero."

"Remember the school!" the priest growled.

The American's mind was immediately filled with the scene imprinted forever in the darkest corner of his memory.

The villagers had voted unanimously not to pay the "taxes" the Shining Path had demanded. The geologist had suggested that if the villagers stood up to the guerrillas, the town would remain safe; the townspeople latched onto the idea and refused to pay the extortion tax, running the would-be tax collector out of town with rakes and stones. When nothing happened for several weeks, it seemed that was the end of it.

Most of the adults were in the fields or searching for gold in the teams the American had organized when the Shining Path guerrillas returned to town. The twelve armed insurgents ignored the old people and women working in the hovels that lined the street and proceeded directly to the diminutive elementary school where Sister Marietta was teaching the children reading.

The first indication of trouble was the pealing of the bell in the crude rock-and-cement *iglisia* next to the school. Everyone who heard it knew something was very wrong, for Father Ramero almost never rang the brittle old bell, even on Easter or Christmas.

Hearing the knell, Lloyd dropped his tools and sample bag and sprinted toward the village, continuing across the rocky slope at breakneck speed and charging down the dusty, deserted main street. No one spoke as he shoved his way through the crowd of weeping parents gathered at the door of the one-room school.

For a moment, everything seemed normal in the darkened interior of the school room. But as his sun-blinded eyes adjusted to the dim light, the rusty smell of blood filled his nostrils.

His face contorted as he inspected the teacher and her fourteen students, all of whom he now saw were bound to their chairs, a macabre travesty of an orderly classroom. The throat of each child, as well as that of the teacher, had been slit. Red tongues dropped from the cuts like watery growths on each chin. The geologist turned and fled in horror, his nausea driving all thought from his brain.

Nobody had blamed Lloyd for what had befallen the school; everyone in the village had been against paying the taxes to the insurgents, but he condemned himself for suggesting the idea in the first place. Harlan Lloyd had pledged a solemn vow to himself never again to allow the Shining Path to harm his village. The tiny lumps of gold he found while prospecting for the mother lode that he knew must be in the area were invested in the purchase of a meager arsenal; as more bits of gold were discovered, he purchased ammunition and taught the villagers to protect themselves.

Now, in the darkness on the slope below the village, the geologist remembered the classroom full of dead children. He realized that if the villagers captured the man, he would suffer a long, torturous death. Although Lloyd knew the terrorist deserved such a death, he didn't hesitate as he raised his rifle, aimed, and fired a single shot.

The .22 bullet crashed through the brain of the wounded guerrilla, bringing an abrupt end to his weeping.

1

Bishop is an ass, Captain Jefferson Davis "Oz" Carson reflected as he spit green mouthwash into the lavatory. *And he gives asses a bad name at that,* he added.

The blond Army pilot straightened up and glanced at himself in the mirror, rubbing his hand across his jaw to be certain he'd cleared every bit of stubble from his chin. Satisfied, he picked up his safety razor and tossed it, along with the still-damp toothbrush, into his shaving kit and zipped it shut.

He carried the kit into the bedroom and crammed it into the flight bag he'd be taking with him to Peru. He eyed the bed and debated whether or not to make it, deciding it didn't matter since no one would be there to know the difference. He grimaced as he remembered Sandy, his ex-wife, and then pushed her from his thoughts.

He plodded into the kitchen and fixed himself a cup of lukewarm instant coffee, which he consumed along with a stale doughnut at the kitchen sink since the table was covered with the parts of a "potato bug" mandolin he'd been assembling on and off over the last month. As he sipped at the bitter brew, his thoughts returned to the unsavory meeting he'd had in his division commander's office at Fort Bragg the day before.

As the pilot had entered Commander Warner's office and saluted, his attention was immediately drawn to the two civilians in the room, but particularly to the icy-eyed man who sat next to the commander's walnut desk, puffing at a cigarette. Oz immediately disliked the looks of the civilian, who wore a black pinstriped suit with a precisely knotted tie.

"Oz," Commander Warner said, returning the salute, "this is Guy Bishop, head of vice-president Decker's secret service staff."

"Mr. Bishop," Oz said, extending his hand as he stepped toward the agent.

Bishop grunted and knocked his cigarette ash into the ashtray in front of him without rising to his feet.

"And this is assistant Secretary of State Sam Valentine," Warner motioned to a hawk-nosed man in a gray pinstriped suit who stood looking out the window.

"I've heard a lot of good things about you," Valentine said with a toothy smile as he approached the pilot and grasped his hand.

"You'll be ferrying the vice-president, his staff, and his contingent of agents into Lima, Peru, for the upcoming meeting there," Warner informed Oz. "Assistant Secretary Valentine and Mr. Bishop have flown in to help us get the kinks worked out of the plans."

"Isn't it a little unusual for us to be ferrying elected officials?" Oz inquired.

"You let us worry about that," Bishop snapped,

before the commander or Valentine could answer. The secret service agent exhaled a cloud of smoke as he continued. "Just because you Night Stalkers usually carry spooks or anti-terr teams doesn't mean you can't do something out of the ordinary. You just get us in there and we'll take care of the rest. Don't try to do any thinking for us."

Oz said nothing, his face a mask. Warner glared at the agent and Valentine unconsciously fumbled with the knot of his tie, a red blush creeping up the back of his neck.

Bishop ignored the three men as he crushed his cigarette butt in the ashtray, then stood, retrieving another cigarette from the pack in his jacket. "I didn't hurt anyone's feelings, did I?" Bishop asked. "I mean, we're all big boys here, right?"

"Some people don't think it's wise to keep their men in the dark," Warner answered. "Or go out of the way to be rude."

"Good advice no doubt, commander," Bishop replied, his artificial smile betrayed by the hardness of his eyes. "I guess I'm too gruff for most people's tastes. I'm sure you and Valentine can brief your man all you want, but as far as I'm concerned," he concluded, jerking his head toward Oz, "all he needs to know is that the vice-president's delegation is headed for Peru. So I'll see him tomorrow when it's time for us to leave. Mr. Valentine, you know where to reach me if you need me before then."

The Secret Service agent strode across the room, opened the door, and left.

Captain Warner swore under his breath. "That chain-smoking SOB is one disagreeable. . . ." He paused to regain his composure and then shook his head.

Valentine nodded. "Bishop varies his approach from being condescending to bullying. But he's one of the best when it comes to security and protecting VIPs, so we give him a little longer leash than would normally be the case."

"Have you ever considered a choke chain?" Oz quipped.

"Yeah, that may be what we need," Valentine agreed, his lips twitching into an apologetic smile.

"Anyway, sit down and let me show you what we've got," Warner told Oz.

The pilot pulled up the chair Bishop had vacated and sat down.

"As you've probably guessed, Captain Carson," Valentine said, "the main concern of the mission to Peru will be getting vice-president Decker in and out without any attacks from the Shining Path—*Sendero Luminoso* as they're called in Spanish."

"How much do you know about the Shining Path, Oz?" Warner asked.

"Not much," the pilot admitted. "It's been a while since I was briefed on them. They're Maoists, right?"

"That's correct," Valentine nodded. "The group's philosophy is based on the obscure writings of a Peruvian Marxist, Jose Carlos Maratequi, whose work influenced Abimael Guzman Reynoso, a professor of philosophy at the University of San Cristobol de Huamanga in Ayacucho. The Ayacucho section of Peru was referred to by the ruling elite as *La Mancha*

India—the Indian Stain—so the Shining Path is, in many ways, the results of racism."

"And racism made the Ayacucho area ripe for Maoism," Oz said.

"Exactly," Valentine nodded. "Guzman adopted the titles of 'Comrade Gonzolo,' and 'The Fourth Sword of Marxism'—the first three swords being Lenin, Stalin, and Mao Tse Tung."

"I've heard the movement is pretty bizarre," Oz remarked.

"To say the least," Warner agreed, shaking a cigarette from the battered pack he'd removed from his pocket. "According to the Army's files, the new version of Maoism mixes military strategy with Andean mysticism for the purpose of recreating the ancient Incan empire."

"That's correct," Valentine agreed. "They refer to the new kingdom as the 'Republic of Tuhuantasuyo'—which will encompass Peru, Ecuador, Bolivia, Chile, and Colombia."

"*That* would certainly upset things in the region," Oz said.

"It sure would," Valentine concurred. "Worse yet, the role model for Guzman's Shining Path is the Khmer Rouge."

"Which killed upward of a third of Kampuchea's population during the purge," Oz said, shaking his head.

"One Shining Path official has been quoted as saying their death list is as thick as the Lima phone directory," Valentine continued.

"How much outside help have they been getting?" Oz asked.

"Surprisingly enough, not much," Valentine answered. "The Shining Path perceives communist movements outside of the Khmer Rouge, North Korea, and Albania as being counterrevolutionary and therefore the enemy. So this is one home-grown communist operation that hasn't been funded by any of the major players in Europe or Asia, but they haven't done too badly on their own.

"Guzman began teaching at the University of San Cristobal de Huamanga in the early 1960s," Valentine continued. "There, he gained control of the philosophy department and quickly worked to create a faculty that fit his needs. By 1978 he'd formed an ideological camp that became the seed group for the *Sendero Luminoso*.

"Before the government of Peru realized what was happening, Guzman had gone underground, along with his closest followers. They formed their plans and engaged in massive recruiting among the Indians in both rural areas and the cities. The basic strategy was to create a unified front of peasants and workers that would gain control of food production, forcing cities and towns to surrender to the guerrillas."

"And they've met with limited success, right?" Warner asked.

"Right," Valentine nodded. "Currently, three Peruvian states—Ayacucho, Huancavelica, and Apurimac—are considered to be 'Sendero Country' since the guerrillas control the areas. They're not pretty players, either.

"Between 1980 and 1990, fifteen thousand people were killed by the Shining Path, and survivors of torture and mutilations push the number of their victims well beyond that. The movement is also responsible for nearly a billion dollars worth of damage in Peru. Adding to all this insanity is the fact that many members of the Shining Path have learned to speak the ancient Inca language and are spreading the rumor that Guzman is the reincarnation of an ancient Incan Indian chief.''

Oz shook his head but said nothing.

"I understand the Peruvian government has not dealt with the situation too effectively, either," Warner remarked.

"I'm afraid that's an accurate assessment," Valentine acknowledged. "The state police, the *Guardia Civil* or paramilitary civil guard, was unable to contain the Shining Path, so in the mid-1980s, the Peruvian Armed Forces' *Guardia Republicana* gained full responsibility for countering the movement."

"And that's resulted in suspension of rights and abuses of power," Warner said.

"Yes," Valentine nodded. "The military created 'Emergency Zones' where human rights have been virtually abolished. Hundreds of mass graves have been found and five thousand people have vanished in the emergency zones. Currently, ten of Peru's twenty-four departments—their state divisions—are declared Emergency Zones, with nearly twenty million people without constitutional guarantees.

"And there are horrible atrocities occurring on both sides," Valentine added. "Soldiers often tie dynamite to suspects and blow them to bits; school children and public officials are the favorite targets of the terrorists."

"Are there any numbers on the membership of the Shining Path?" Oz asked. "There must be a lot of them to rack up so many victims."

"In 1990," Valentine answered, "the Peruvian Investigative Police, the *Policia de Investigaciones*, put the number of Shining Path members at thirty thousand, with three to four thousand actively involved in guerrilla activities."

Warner whistled.

"Of course the Shining Path puts its numbers higher," Valentine continued. "One hundred thousand, with thirty thousand actively involved."

"Either way, it's a *very* large guerrilla organization," Oz said.

"And," Warner added, "if the file I've seen is correct, there's also a twist in who's giving aid to the Peruvian government."

"Right," the assistant secretary of state nodded. "Because of the Shining Path's antagonism toward the USSR, the Soviets supplied the government of Peru with military advisors and weapons throughout the 1980s. Consequently, Soviet diplomats and military advisors have been targets—as have the Chinese and Cubans.

"An anti-guerrilla strike force created by the Soviets—the *Cinchis*—is under the *Guardia Civil*," Valentine continued. "Although originally organized by the U.S. Green Berets in the 1960s, they became effective only with Soviet training. Advisors included Russian Spetsnaz units who apparently often fight alongside the *Cinchis*. To counter the Soviet help, the Shining Path turned to helping Colombian drug traffickers believed to belong to the Medellín drug cartel smuggle their drugs into the Soviet Union via Spain.

"Which leads to the final irony," the assistant secretary added. "During the last days of the Cold War, U.S. Drug Enforcement Agency units often fought alongside *Cinchis* and Spetsnaz personnel in the Huallaga Valley at the northeastern edge of Peru, where the majority of the drug traffic seems to be located."

"Any other players we should be aware of?" Warner asked.

"I'm afraid so," Valentine answered. "The Rodrigo Franco Command—composed of ruling leftists in the APRA party—the police, soldiers, and the *Tupac Amaru,* which is a less radical Marxist terrorist group based in a few rural areas. Finally there's the ruling American Popular Revolutionary Alliance party, or APRA, calling for public ownership of basic industries and equal rights for all citizens. They've been buying small arms and light weapons from North Korea, apparently to fight the Shining Path, but possibly to forestall a military coup as well. Into this mess add runaway inflation—as high as 400 percent per month—a low standard of living, and the lack of foreign companies investing in the area because of all the problems."

"And you want to take the vice-president of the United States into the middle of all that?" Oz asked.

"I'm afraid that's right," Valentine smiled ruefully.

"It's no wonder Bishop didn't want to stick around while we briefed you, Oz," Warner snickered.

"Whether or not the U.S. government can do anything to help Peru remains to be seen," Valentine admitted. "But the State Department wants to try something instead of just sitting around while Peru goes down the drain.

"Because the *Policia de Investigaciones* has been hearing rumors that an assassination attempt will be made on the vice-president's life, the Secret Service has insisted the last leg of the journey be made in an armed American helicopter capable of repulsing an attack."

"The short of it is that the government wanted the best, and—as far as the Army's concerned—you're it," Warner told Oz. "Now let's get to the details of your trip before you get a swollen head."

Then the three men had analyzed the plans for moving the vice-president from the Peruvian air force base to the secret meeting place where a series of talks would be conducted with the president of Peru.

Even if everything goes as planned, I'll be real glad when this mission's completed, Oz thought as he finished his doughnut and set the empty coffee mug into the pile of dirty dishes in the kitchen sink. The pilot returned to the bedroom and retrieved his flight bag, then headed out the back door, locking it behind him.

As usual, Hell was nowhere to be seen; Oz checked to be sure there was an ample supply of dog food—the feline's favorite meal—in her bowl. At least the food might keep the neighbors' birds safe for the duration, the pilot mused as he traversed the short distance to the detached garage.

He tossed the flight bag into the empty back seat of his Acura Integra GS, then climbed into the front and started the car's engine, which immediately purred to life. Backing out of the driveway, he headed for O.T.'s.

Traveling eight minutes north on Highway 24, he turned onto a side road and stopped in front of the warrant officer's light gray ranch house and honked the horn twice.

As he sat waiting, Oz checked his watch, then searched the oaks that surrounded the house for the gray squirrel that chattered noisily in one of the trees. A moment later, Harvey "O.T." Litwin came lumbering out the front door, his shaved head gleaming in the early morning sunlight.

The middle-aged warrant officer threw his flight bag and jacket into the back seat, opened the car door, and slung his heavy frame into the passenger seat. "Guess I'm ready to go, but I won't be sure until I wake up," he joshed as he slammed the door and buckled his seatbelt.

They backtracked a mile down Highway 24, turned west onto Manchester Road, and headed for Pope Air Force Base north of Fort Bragg, North Carolina, where they'd be boarding a C-141B "Starlifter" cargo plane.

"I don't have a real good feeling about this mission," O.T. admitted as they approached the checkpoint at the entrance of the air force base.

Oz said nothing.

The Lockheed C-141B carried the army flight and ground crew, secret service agents, the vice-president and his staff, and an air force security squad on its upper deck; below, in the belly of the cargo plane, the partially disassembled Sikorsky MH-60K helicopter waited, secured in place with heavy, steel cables.

The vice-president spent much of the journey studiously reading through a stack of documents and reports; his staff engaged in a heated debate about South American foreign policy during the first half hour of the trip and then sat glumly or catnapped in their seats the remainder of the long flight.

O.T. and Lieutenant Chad "Death Song" Norton, the co-pilot of the MH-60K that would fly vice-president Decker on the last leg of his trip into Lima, played several mile-high chess games on the tiny magnetic board the warrant officer always had stashed in his belongings whenever he traveled. SP4 Mike Luger, Oz's crew chief, huddled in one of the net chairs, trying valiantly not to get sick as the plane occasionally lurched from air turbulence.

The C-141B voyaged in bright sunlight, above the cotton clouds that shrouded the earth below. The pylon-mounted turbo jets beneath the plane's high wings droned loudly, making it hard for those inside to carry on conversations.

The air force pilot in the cockpit had set the auto pilot to barber-pole the C-141B, flying them at the maximum speed of 495 kilometers-per-hour to trim their trip to 11 hours. When they neared Lima, the pilot took the plane off autopilot and received permission to land on a Peruvian government air strip; after verifying there were no Indians—private planes in the vicinity of the runway—the pilot slam-dunked the C-141B to minimize their exposure to a possible rocket attack mounted by guerrilla forces.

The quick descent nauseated Luger, who frantically clutched a barf bag over his mouth as the aircraft landed at its maximum safe descent speed, its ten wheels screeching on the runway with a shudder.

Following the control tower's directions, the pilot taxied to the northern side of the tarmac where a detachment of Peruvian jeeps mounted with Browning machine guns surrounded the jet.

The squad of U.S. air force security guards bounded out of the C-141B's open cargo door, equipped with night vision goggles, full combat gear, and armed with M16 rifles, an FN Minimi, and an M203 grenade launcher. The American security contingent ignored the Peruvian jeeps and quickly fanned out into the cool night to ensure to their own satisfaction that the area was indeed secure.

Once the air force sergeant in charge of the security force signaled the all-clear, the air force crew members inside the belly of the C-141B began assisting the army ground team in off-loading the MH-60K helicopter from the hold of the cargo jet. The men labored with practiced precision, carefully freeing the chopper from its steel bonds and rolling the machine onto the darkened runway still warm from the sun's rays.

The secret service agents, armed with Micro Uzi and TEC-9K machine pistols, escorted the vice-president and his staff to a waiting limousine while Oz and his crew climbed out of the jet into the chilly night behind the last of the agents.

"Luger," O.T. said, patting the woozy crew chief on the back, "the army would be real proud of the way you've managed to get your skin a nice shade of olive green."

"I certainly understand why the pope kisses the ground whenever he gets off a jet," Luger quipped, his face looking paler than usual.

"Please don't kiss the ground and make us look bad," Oz deadpanned.

"Hey, I thought we were supposed to take the VP into Lima," Death Song asserted, pointing to the secret service agents climbing into the waiting limousine.

"We are," Oz informed his co-pilot, "but they're going to whisk him and his entourage away for awhile and then return just before we take off. Bishop thinks we're all sitting ducks here on the airfield."

"Somehow that's not too comforting," O.T. remarked.

No one spoke as the black limousine sped into the night with a squeal of rubber tires on the warm concrete of the tarmac.

"They're coming," the lookout warned in Quechua, the ancient language of the Incas.

Enrico Zurita lifted his AKM rifle to unfold its metal stock. "They're coming," he repeated. "Pass the word to fire only after I start shooting at the convoy."

Zurita had been nineteen the last time he had engaged in an ambush, seven years ago. His hand whipped over his black hair and trailed down his long ponytail as he remembered how green he'd been—not as experienced as even the newest of the rebels he now led.

Like other Peruvian Indians, Zurita had been the victim of racism more times than he cared to remember, a result of the class system instituted by the Spanish in the seventeenth century; their system continued to permeate Peruvian society to this very day. Even as a child it had been simple for Zurita to understand: those with light, European skins were the haves and those with swarthy skins like his own were the have-nots. There was nothing complicated about the class system in Peru.

The upper class had always been meager in numbers, but throughout the centuries after Pizarro had captured and killed Atahualpa, the last of the Inca king's sons, the Spaniards and their heirs had managed to keep the huge lower class of native Americans poor. Only the half-breeds—the *mestizos*—were occasionally able to rise to become part of the ruling class; and even that had been rare during recent years.

Although a diminutive middle class had developed during the mid-1900s, the changes were too slow to suit Zurita. All he could see were the rich continuing to grow richer by exploiting the lower classes. It was self-evident that the cessation of discrimination and exploitation was not going to materialize during his lifetime, his children's, or his grandchildren's unless something was done to break the system.

So Zurita had been more than willing to throw in his lot with the *Sendero Luminoso* when he'd first heard one of the rebels speak to a crowd that had collected on a dusty corner in his village. The speaker promised equality, a termination to the rule of the Spaniards' descendants, and a return of the Incan Empire that had once constituted the greatest power in South America.

Zurita still didn't like the violence that seemed to be integral to bringing about the changes promised by the Shining Path, but he knew it was the only way to usher in a semblance of equality for his fellow native Americans. And because the violence was necessary, Zurita tried to learn it as efficiently as was humanly possible. Little by little, he hardened himself to the savagery and soon became one of the leaders in Shining Path operations centered around his native city of Cajamaroa.

Now he had been selected by Comrade Gonzolo himself, the reincarnated *Sapa Inca,* to spearhead their efforts in Lima, which were aimed at keeping the APRA from forming an alliance with the United States.

The first stage of this plan entailed the securing of heavy weapons for fighting the American and Peruvian soldiers head on. While the Shining Path did wonders solely with dynamite, readily available with the many mining operations throughout Peru, the operation Zurita was in charge of called for precise power. They needed the weapons being shipped today in a modest truck convoy.

"There!" the messenger told Zurita, pointing along the winding trail bordered on either side by the cliffs where the Shining Path guerrillas were hidden.

"I see it," Zurita acknowledged, clicking the safety on the right side of the AKM's receiver from "safe" to semiauto. "Quit waving your arms around or they'll see us, too."

The chastened messenger dropped in back of the boulder and readied his own rifle.

There was only one crude road between Lima and Cajamaroa and, like the majority of roads in Peru, this one was gravel; the canyon where the rebels had laid their trap was barely wide enough for one truck to pass through. As the engine of the lead government truck seemed to groan, its driver shifted to a lower gear to climb through the pass and the noise echoed from the rocky walls as he drove between them.

Zurita's timing had to be perfect if he was going

to trap the three trucks. If he attacked too soon or too late, one or even two of the trucks might escape. Worse yet, once a truck was clear of the pass, the driver could radio for help. It was unlikely any of the government helicopter gunships were in the area; but if one happened to be around, the tables could quickly be turned and Zurita and his men could become the hunted rather than the hunters.

The truck lumbered into sight, smoke bellowing from the muffler mounted on the side of its cab. A machine gun installed on a rail above the top of the cab was unmanned, the gunner sitting inside the cab laughing as he helped himself to another swig from his bottle.

Where are the other two trucks? Zurita wondered agitatedly as the first vehicle thundered below him. The rebel leader hadn't expected the drivers to let themselves get so spread out, and he couldn't afford not to attack, gunship or not: the weapons were essential if the guerrillas were to disrupt the U.S./Peruvian conference the next day in Lima.

There was another belch of smoke and the second and third trucks toiled their way up the incline into sight. Zurita heaved a sigh of relief and raised his rifle to center the attached scope on the driver of the second truck. Although his rifle wasn't accurate enough to assure his hitting the driver, he decided to try it anyway since his first shot would be the signal to his men to initiate their attack.

His finger squeezed the trigger and the rifle spit fire, lightly kicking against his shoulder.

The windshield of the truck below him spalled and the driver, though not hit by the .30-caliber bullet that crashed into the cab, lifted his hands to shield his eyes from the glass chips that were cutting into his face. During the few seconds his hands left the steering wheel, the tires of his truck locked into a rut and the vehicle careened off the edge of the road and dropped into the low ditch alongside it. The driver and the troops inside the truck were thrown helter-skelter as the vehicle came to an abrupt halt.

A fraction of a second later, the lead truck was peppered with a shower of gunfire from automatic weapons on either side of the trail. A charge of dynamite detonated at the top of the ridge behind the last truck as the driver slammed to a halt and tried to reverse his direction. He slammed on his brakes again as tons of rock and gravel slid over the narrow road behind him, effectively cutting off his escape.

The gunner in the cab of the rear truck scrambled up behind the FN MAG T1 machine gun mounted atop the cab and jerked back the charging lever on the gun. He commenced firing at the few guerrillas he could see along the ridge above him. The driver eased the truck forward after grinding through the gears, searching for first.

Bullets from the FN machine gun zinged past Zurita's head, creating loud, sonic cracks. A watery thud accompanied the cracks and Zurita was splattered with warm liquid. Glancing toward his messenger, he saw the man fall, the top of his head missing.

Zurita ducked behind the boulder as the machine gunner in the truck below again raked the ridge with a long string of shots. The rebel leader slapped the selector on his rifle into its automatic position and rose to align the AKM on the cab of the truck.

The government machine gunner appeared in the crosshairs of Zurita's rifle scope, vanished when the truck bounced forward, and was reacquired when the rebel leader expertly followed his target. This time the machine gunner remained in the crosshairs.

The guerilla leader discharged his firearm with a short rap on the trigger.

The sight picture of the scope was lost with the recoil of Zurita's rifle during the shuddering thrust of automatic fire. Then he lowered the scope to again view the cab of the truck.

Zurita found the machine gunner was gone, a bloody smear on the windshield signifying that the burst from the AKM had found its intended target. The rebel leader followed the moving truck once more, this time aiming at the driver. He pulled the trigger and the man at the wheel jerked spasmodically, falling a fraction of a second after three bullets stitched the windshield in front of him.

Satisfied the worst of the resistance was past, Zurita rose and watched the unfolding battle below him, occasionally sighting through his scope to fire at the few government troops who offered any effective counterfire.

Taking advantage of a lull in the shooting as many of the guerrillas exhausted their rifle magazines, six soldiers in the lead truck jumped from the rear of the vehicle and dashed toward the second truck in an effort to escape the heavy fire that had been raining down upon them.

Renewed gunfire erupted from the hills on either side of them as the fleeing soldiers were targeted, dropping one by one into the dusty gravel.

Another explosion rocked the valley.

Zurita stared at the fireball that crackled above the rear truck, engulfed now in flames, and realized the vehicle must have been leaking fuel. He remained unconcerned, however, since he knew that only the two trucks in front of it contained the weapons they needed.

Abruptly, the gunfire from the government troops ended with the explosion, and Zurita smiled to himself when he discerned what had happened. The soldiers assumed the rebels possessed weapons capable of destroying their trucks. White bandages tied to the barrels of rifles appeared from the two remaining trucks as if by magic; the crude banners waved frantically in the dusty air while the frightened soldiers remained hidden in the cabs of the vehicles.

Zurita waited a moment and then ordered a cease-fire. All but one of his men immediately quit firing. "Cease fire!" the rebel leader repeated.

The mountains became ominously silent.

Zurita cupped his hands around his mouth and shouted in Spanish to the soldiers below. "Step away from the trucks." There was no movement other than the flags that continued their frenzied waving. "We'll let you go unharmed if you surrender," the rebel leader promised when he saw they were too fearful to leave the security of the trucks.

One of the troopers carrying a makeshift truce flag cautiously stepped away from the center truck. He hesitated for a second, then resolutely paced away from the truck to stand in the center of the open road.

"It's all right," Zurita yelled again. "We will not

harm you. Throw down your guns. Move away from the trucks."

More of the soldiers appeared, surrounding the first trooper.

Zurita signaled his four best men who immediately descended the steep hillside to the trucks, half skating, half sliding on the seat of their pants, rifles at the ready.

The four rebels rapidly checked the lead and second trucks to be sure no soldiers remained hidden in them and then they inspected the last truck, which was burning furiously, raising a black cloud that drifted above the face of the cliff.

One of the four raised his rifle and waved an all-clear.

"Head down and get the trucks rolling!" Zurita hollered to the remaining revolutionaries, this time in Quechua.

The twenty-four Shining Path guerrillas hidden among the boulders rose and slid down the steep banks of the canyon on either side of the road. Zurita followed them, raising a cloud of dust as he descended to the roadway.

"Get away from the bodies and get into the trucks," Zurita ordered several of the younger men who were searching one of the bloody corpses for booty. The rebel leader ignored the dead man lying in the dust, crossing toward the cluster of soldiers cowering under the watchful eye of Zurita's guards.

"Do we kill them?" whispered Rui Garcia, Zurita's right-hand man.

"No," Zurita responded. "One day they may join us."

"But comrade—"

"No one else dies unless they try to stop us," Zurita insisted.

"As you say," Garcia replied, not meeting his leader's eyes.

"Be careful, Comrade Garcia, that you do not develop a taste for blood," Zurita cautioned. "Death is a tool, not an end in itself."

Garcia smiled grimly and nodded.

"Get the soldiers out of the way so we can drive past," Zurita ordered, not waiting for the command to be executed. He turned and briskly walked back to the trucks. "Get going," he ordered the drivers who sat in the two vehicles.

The lead driver twisted the key in the ignition and the truck sputtered to life, a cloud of blue smoke choking from its muffler. As the second vehicle was mobilized, the two trucks resumed their trip up the steep incline, under the command of the Shining Path guerrillas.

Being on a military base, the vice-president's secret service agents, led by Guy Bishop, didn't even attempt to hide the fact that they were heavily armed. Two members of the eight-man team carried Colt "Commando" carbines with eleven-and-a-half-inch barrels; each gun sported twin Thermold 45-round magazines loaded with duplex cartridges containing two bullets per cartridge.

The other six agents each carried a modified machine pistol. Five held Micro Uzi submachine guns; Decker carried a nickel-colored TEC-9K. Little bigger than a pistol, the machine pistols had compensators milled into the ends of their short barrels. The Uzis held thirty-two rounds while the TEC-9K accepted a similar nickel-plated magazine. All six of the machine pistols were chambered for the .354 Smith & Wesson cartridge which—although just slightly longer than a 9mm Luger cartridge—boasted the power of a .357 Magnum.

In addition, most of the agents brandished Beretta 92s chambered for the .354 S&W cartridge, concealing the pistols in shoulder harnesses under their suit jackets. The vice-president and the agents wore Kevlar ballistic vests capable of stopping most submachine gun bullets as well as buckshot.

"Mr. Decker," Bishop addressed the vice-president, "I've received an all-clear from Captain Carson and the air force security team. Are you ready to head for the chopper?"

"We're ready if you are," Decker replied in the fulsome tones of a radio evangelist.

With Bishop's signal, the chauffeur flipped the switch that unlocked the doors of the limousine, and four agents spilled out, squinting in the early morning sunlight to scrutinize their surroundings for potential hazards. A thumbs-up sign was soon forthcoming.

"Go!" Bishop ordered those who remained in the limousine. The rest of the party immediately departed the armored sanctuary, and within seconds the agents had formed a human shield around the vice-president and his three staff members, herding them toward the waiting MH-60K at the center of the airfield.

Decker, a one-time presidential hopeful who, during a backroom compromise, had become the nominee's running mate, ducked his head and squinted to prevent the swishing blades of the helicopter from blowing grit into his contact lenses. The Floridian grimaced as the man-made tempest of the rotors disordered his carefully combed snowy-white hair.

As they approached the chopper, Decker noted the aircraft's heavy armament. Six wicked barrels of a Minigun poked from the gunners door on each side, while three weapons pods perched on the pylons stretching from its fuselage. One of the pods sported a dual machine gun, while the other two encased an array of rockets with explosive warheads. The fourth pylon pod, Decker knew, carried an electronic countermeasures system capable of jamming radar and radio transmissions, as well as countering most types of guided missiles that might be launched at the MH-60K. The vice-president was impressed with the no-nonsense look of the formidable machine.

As the knot of agents and politicians neared the chopper, the side door slid open and O.T., his face half-hidden by the sun visor of his helmet, extended his hand. "Welcome aboard, Mr. vice-president," he shouted over the gale of the blades, helping the dignitary climb in.

"Thanks," Decker bellowed, grasping the warrant officer's hand and scrambling aboard.

"Sit right here, sir," O.T. directed once they were inside, "and please fasten your shoulder harness so you don't bounce around in flight. We'll be flying low and fast."

Although the vice-president chuckled, Bishop inspected O.T. frostily as the warrant officer crossed back to close and lock the side door behind the last of the agents, thereby encasing the passengers in the armored skin of the MH-60K. O.T. turned and waited another few seconds, surveying his passengers to ensure that each one had fastened his shoulder harness.

"Come on, let's get going!" Bishop yelled. "Are we going to sit out here in the open until somebody takes a potshot at us?"

"Okay," O.T. answered mildly, realizing the agent was every bit as abrasive as Oz had said he was. The seasoned trooper made his way forward to the gunners cabin to take his position opposite Luger, who sat behind his Minigun. O.T. snapped the jack of his helmet mike into the intercom system and spoke to Oz. "All aboard, captain. Bishop's real antsy for take-off."

"And wasn't afraid to express his impatience, I bet," Oz responded from the cockpit. The pilot inspected the sunny sky over the airstrip to be sure it was clear and then, since the pre-flight checklist had been completed and clearance for takeoff granted by the air traffic controller, he lifted the collective pitch lever in his left fist. The rotors above him changed their pitch angle and increased in speed with a furious thumping. "Death Song, watch the radar and be ready with countermeasures."

"I'll be ready," the American Indian co-pilot assured him. "Shall I arm our weapons?"

"Negative," the pilot answered as the chopper leaped into the air amid a cloud of fine dust. "I'm more interested in avoiding trouble than shooting our way out." The idea of being able to fight off an attack sounded good, the pilot reflected, but it wouldn't be too practical once they got over Lima. He didn't care to imagine what the news services would make of it if a stray U.S. rocket or a burst from their machine guns were to smash into a residential area.

"Countermeasures are on standby," Death Song announced, studying the multi-mode radar and forward-looking infrared viewer.

Oz rotated the chopper in the air to align them onto their course toward Lima. As the dark MH-60K wheeled and climbed higher, its shadow raced across the surface of the tarmac as if headed for a different location. Then the penumbra started to follow the chopper as it accelerated.

The pilot continued to shove the control column forward so their speed was rapidly increasing as they cleared the barbed-wire perimeter of the airstrip and then traversed the nearby shantytown.

Despite the ragged look of the haphazardly built huts, the village was neat and—oddly enough—sanctioned by the Peruvian government, which encouraged the upwardly mobile squatters to work hard and save money for permanent structures rather than sink it into rent payments. In the meantime, the government supplied water and sewer systems to such *pueblos jovenes,* or "young towns," to maintain the health of the workers living there.

Oz shivered and adjusted the heat module in the control console sitting between him and Death Song. Although Lima was merely twelve degrees south of the Equator, the cold ocean current along its coast and the chilly air which drifted off the Andes kept the coastal area cool. It was presently 58° Fahrenheit outside and the expected high for the day was only seventy-nine, even though it was mid-summer, and the air was dry, making the atmosphere felt chillier since it leached moisture from the skin. Oz had heard that many of the coastal areas actually experienced less rainfall than parts of the Sahara desert.

"I'm engaging the TF/TA," the pilot informed the navigator as they cleared the shantytown. He flipped on the terrain following/terrain avoidance radar that was coupled to the controls of the chopper, enabling them to stay below any radar surveillance and reducing their chances of being sighted by guerrillas on the flight to Lima.

Once the TF/TA was engaged, the chopper dropped closer to the rocky hills below, skimming the surface of the earth as they raced toward their destination. At daybreak, Oz had thought the rocky foothills around the air base were covered with snow; in fact, it was fine, gray sand that blew and drifted around the outcroppings of stone.

The pilot checked the instruments to be sure the MH-60K was functioning properly, paying special attention to the vertical situation display, which listed all aspects of the flight path, horizon, and heading of the chopper, along with its radar altitude and the pitch of its blades. Satisfied everything was operating correctly, he addressed Death Song. "Connect us with Mother Hen so we can apprise the States of our status."

"Just a sec," the co-pilot responded, tapping the code into the on-board computer that supplied the uplink to the communications satellite high above Central America. The helicopter lurched down a steep incline as Death Song spoke. "We've got a link; the COMSAT is interrogating our computer now." He paused for a moment and then added, "We're locked in. You can go ahead."

The pilot triggered the radio switch on the control column in his right hand. "This is Shining Path One calling Mother Hen. Over."

"This is Mother Hen," Captain Warner's voice came back, sounding as if he were next door instead of on the next continent. "How're you doing with your schedule? Over."

"Right on the money, Mother Hen," Oz answered. "Everything's going as planned and we've experienced no problems—other than a mouthy agent. Over."

"That I can believe," Warner laughed, recalling how Bishop had behaved during the initial briefing. "We don't have any new info for you on this end. I'll talk to you after you get your eggs into the basket. Good luck. Over and out."

Oz toggled off the radio and glanced through the chin window at another huge shantytown they were traveling over. Some of the people who lived in the ramshackle houses were pointing and waving at the black chopper as it raced above them. One of the hills adjoining the makeshift community was a cascade of crimson and white where weavers were displaying their colorful blankets and ponchos for passing tourists. As the chopper hurtled over the villagers, the Army pilot checked the VSD and then spoke on the intercom. "Our LZ's just a few minutes away. If anybody's going to try anything, this is probably when they'll do it. Remember, we will *not* return any ground fire unless we have to."

Within minutes, they were crossing over the outskirts of Lima, headed toward the taller buildings that sprang skyward in the renewed northern edge of the city. He glanced at the horizontal situation display to check the map projection and navigation reference points which the 1750A/J73 dual mission computers updated to show their position over the city. "That's our LZ straight ahead, isn't it?" he asked Death Song.

"That's it," the navigator replied.

"O.T.," Oz called over the intercom. "Have the dogs ready. We're headed in."

"I'll alert them," O.T. answered.

On the streets far below the city, the American chopper's blades echoed off the buildings and rumbled down the canyons of the streets to be lost in the reverberation of heavy trucks carrying bales of cotton and cars that choked the air with exhaust fumes.

One intent observer watched the American MH-60K from the street below as it circled its landing zone. Enrico Zurita studied the chopper as it crossed over the busy thoroughfare and approached the roof of the Peruvian Transamerican Bank building like a giant dragonfly.

The streets ringing the building were filled with *Guardia Civil* barricades and cars, their lights strobing a frantic warning that the area was under their protection. Guards wearing camouflaged uniforms and steel helmets that glistened in the sunlight paced the barricades, their AKM rifles held ready for any possible danger.

On the buildings opposite the meeting site, soldiers with Steyr SSG bolt-action sniper rifles could barely be seen as they kept watch over the rooftops and streets. Zurita's informants had told him machine gun emplacements were hidden within the facades of the surrounding buildings.

"They've prepared well," Zurita remarked to Rui Garcia.

"The sky and streets belong to them," the other n agreed.

"But the underworld is ours," Zurita smiled. comrades ready?"

Garcia nodded. "The Americans will never suspect anything until it's too late."

Zurita grinned again. This blow against the imperialists would bring the day of freedom much closer for his people.

Harlan Lloyd ran a hand through his red beard and tried to think.

He was convinced that the gold nuggets that he and the village teams had found were eluvial placer deposits. If he was right, the mother lode from which the nuggets had broken away was somewhere near their village and he was almost as certain that the vein must be in the horned cliff above Piton. But thus far, neither he nor the villagers had enjoyed any luck in finding the source of the tiny nuggets.

There was one route left; that would be to start mining operations. Lloyd didn't relish the idea for two reasons: the expense and scale of the operation and the need to bring in people from outside the village.

Even if he could scrape the money together to hire workers or convince a company to invest in the operation for him, there was no guarantee that the gold wasn't alluvial, perhaps having been carried into the area by the action of water or ice. So the work might end with nothing to show for it. And when he was finished, the village would likely be one big pile of worthless rubble as well.

Yet he remained convinced there was a huge vein somewhere in the area, if only they could find it.

He dropped his rock hammer and sample bag in disgust and sat down on a boulder. *Maybe it doesn't make any difference,* he told himself. He wasn't sure he wanted to find the gold; the villagers seemed content with their lives the way they were; the little money they earned by selling their meager harvests of coffee beans took care of their most pressing needs.

And money didn't seem so important to him anymore, either.

It had been five years since he'd come to Piton to get rich quick. He'd studied NASA satellite photos and become convinced there was gold to be found in the Andean mountains in the area where Piton was located. After buying mineral rights from the government with the last of his savings, he'd come to live in the village to discover his fortune.

And when did I quit being a Yankee and become one of them? he wondered.

When he'd married Maria? Or was it when he'd started teaching them to fight off the guerrillas who came around periodically to beat taxes from them?

Or when he'd gotten their children killed in the school?

Lloyd trembled at the thought.

"Senor Lloyd!" someone called.

The geologist glanced up to see Father Ramero running toward him, holding his robes high to keep from tripping, his dark, hairy legs exposed. To the American, the father looked somehow birdlike, like an escaped ostrich flitting across a rocky plane, Lloyd decided. "What's going on?" the American asked, suppressing a grin at the priest's disheveled appearance.

"Ernesto sighted a column of guerrillas coming toward the village!"

"Are you sure? Last week he sent us on that wild goose—"

"He's certain this time. They have guns. And some type of larger weapon as well."

Lloyd had expected the next attack to come at night, but there seemed to be no doubt that it was to occur instead this morning. He sprang to his feet. "Let's go!"

The old church bell continued to peel, becoming progressively weaker as the crack in its surface spread. Lloyd sprinted into the center of the tiny hamlet, gasping for breath in the thin air for a few moments before he was able to speak. "Ernesto," he panted, addressing one of the villagers who anxiously awaited him. "You and your team take the machine gun we captured from the rebels to the top of the *punta*. And remember to aim and shoot short bursts or you'll exhaust your ammunition before you know it."

Ernesto nodded in agreement and he and the three riflemen who would guard his flank lifted the Czech ZB30 LMG and headed for the ridge overlooking the village, where an improvised machine gun post that resembled an eagle's nest was perched in the rocks.

"Jose," Lloyd said, addressing the squat man who carried an old Mossberg 500 pump shotgun. "Are the new dynamite charges in place?"

"Only the front trail. We didn't have time—"

"Can't be helped now. Father Ramero?"

"My team's got it," the priest pledged, beckoning to the nun and two men who would act as his guards and assistants in setting off the improvised mines along the trails approaching Piton.

Father Ramero's team hurried away as Lloyd surveyed the remaining villagers crowded around him. "Mothers with children get to the church immediately," he instructed. "Those with captured AKMs, remember to keep them on semiauto and *aim* so your shots count. Let's get into our positions behind the wall. They'll be here any minute."

The geologist lifted the worn binoculars Maria had brought to him from their hut and peered out at the trail leading to the village. He could discern fifteen rebels approaching, skulking in a crouch with their rifles ready, taking advantage of the boulders to hide behind.

"Soon they will be in our traps," Maria whispered, flicking the cross-bolt safety on her Ruger rifle into its fire position.

"With any luck," Lloyd agreed absently.

"With God's providence," Father Ramero corrected as he fingered the blasting machine.

As Lloyd continued studying the trail, he couldn't quite believe the rebels would be foolish enough to engage in a frontal assault in the middle of the day. That could only mean. . . .

That these men were a diversionary force and there must be others, he suddenly realized.

He swept the hills with his binoculars, frantically

searching the rocks and scrub brush for guerrillas on the hillside. Where were they?

"Senor Lloyd," one of the boy messengers whispered as he dropped to the dirt beside the geologist.

"What have you got, Saluo?" Lloyd asked the skinny child.

"Fourteen of the *Sendero Luminoso* are running up the west slope. They're off the trail."

"Climb up to Ernesto and tell him to ignore the guerrillas on the front trail—we'll take care of them. Tell him to concentrate on the men on the west slope. And tell his spotters to watch the other trails."

Saluo nodded and scampered away like a rabbit toward the *punta* towering behind them.

Suddenly the rattle of automatic rifles to the east of the village was heard, answered by the louder thunder of the Ernesto's machine gun atop the *punta*. The battle for the village had begun.

Oz circled high above the landing pad painted on the asphalt roof of the Transamerican Bank building. The MH-60K headed west, its shadow preceding it, first scrambling up the sides of buildings, vanishing over their tops, and then reappearing on the streets below as the chopper circled.

In the passenger compartment of the helicopter, Bishop again positioned his men to form a human shield around the vice-president as he disembarked from the aircraft.

A gust of wind jerked at the aircraft as it swung over the roof of the building, but Oz swiftly compensated for it, kicking a rudder pedal to align the chopper's tail rotor blades to present the least amount of danger to those exiting the helicopter.

As the MH-60K hovered above the pad, Oz pulled on the control column to center the landing gear. He then gradually lowered the collective pitch lever in his left hand, decreasing the angle of the four main blades, and the helicopter dropped toward the roof of the tall building.

As the wheels of the chopper neared the asphalt

surface, the ground cushion effect came into play, causing the helicopter to stop its descent. To compensate, Oz carefully lowered the collective pitch lever and dropped the last few feet toward the landing pad. When the wheels touched, he shoved the lever full down and adjusted the throttle to keep the speed of the blades in their proper range. With the wind attempting to shove the MH-60K to the side, the pilot also tapped the right pedal with his foot to maintain his heading. The chopper bounced slightly on its hydraulic landing gear to announce the fact that they were firmly planted on the landing pad.

Oz studied the Peruvian guards who were approaching the helicopter while their counterparts stood near the elevator shaft leading from the roof. The burly sentinels carried oiled AKM rifles that gleamed in the bright sunlight, reminding the American pilot of his days in Vietnam when the Vietcong had often been armed with similar Chinese-made guns.

He realized solemnly that just one traitor among the Peruvian guards could kill the vice-president instantly.

"O.T.," Oz called on the intercom, "remind our dogs to keep their heads down and stay clear of the tail rotors."

"Yes, sir, will do," the warrant officer replied. He stepped into the passenger compartment where Bishop and his men were waiting impatiently at the door.

Five of the secret service agents had their Micro Uzis packed in special briefcases designed to be opened at a moment's notice; Bishop had a similar case, but he carried his lighter, modified TEC-9K in his. From a distance, an observer would conclude that only the agents with Colt Commando carbines were part of the security force, while Bishop and the five other agents must part of the vice-president's staff.

O.T. stopped at the side door and turned to the passengers. "Watch out for the blades overhead and avoid the tail rotors."

"We'll stay clear of 'em," Decker promised, smoothing his long, snowy hair with one hand while gripping his briefcase so tightly with the other that his knuckles turned white. "Everyone ready?" he asked his two staff members.

The two nodded and swallowed, knowing they'd be heading out of the chopper, ready or not.

O.T. grasped the release lever on the side door. "Ready?" he asked Bishop.

"Crack her open," the agent ordered evenly.

O.T. tugged the lever and unlocked the door with a loud click, then threw it rearward on its runners. As the bright sunlight soaked into the compartment, everyone blinked.

Bishop and the agents leaped out of the helicopter, checking in all directions, with their briefcases held at odd angles to be opened rapidly for retrieval of the weapons inside if necessary. The two agents carrying Commando carbines took positions at the front and rear of the delegation, their guns held with the barrels pointing upward, ready to be brought into play instantly if they were needed. The Peruvian guards, perceiving the intensity of the trained agents, unconsciously stepped back to give the Americans room.

O.T. watched until the group was ushered into

the elevator located at the end of the roof; then he slid the side door of the MH-60K home so it latched and crossed forward to the gunners cabin and plugged into the intercom. "The vice-president is in the building and we're secure back here," he reported to Oz.

"Let's get into the air then," the pilot responded, conscious of their vulnerability on top of the open roof. "How's the radar, Death Song?"

"We've got two choppers coming in about a mile behind us—probably Peruvian military—and lots of activity at the commercial airport. It's all clear ahead of us."

"Keep a sharp lookout, everyone," Oz ordered as he pulled up on the collective pitch lever and the helicopter leaped into the air. He circled the Transamerican Bank building whose glass and polished aluminum surface reflected the dark green helicopter like a giant mirror. Satisfied that all was as it should be, Oz flipped his radio to the secret service frequency and toggled on the radio. "This is SP-1 to the babysitter. All's clear out here; how's it look from your end? Over."

Bishop's voice answered, "Everything's fine in here. We'll call you when we need a pick-up. Over and out."

Oz aligned the aircraft onto a course that would return them to the military airstrip, where they were to remain until the meetings had been completed. He glanced through the chin window and thought, for a terrible moment, that he'd seen a rocket launch.

Before he could react, he realized it was simply steam coming from an open pipe on the street far below—likely a dry cleaner or some industrial job, he decided, his heart still pounding. He realized then how uptight he was.

But while he'd seen a few pilots crash and burn because they were too cautious, most went down when they were daydreaming or taking their safety for granted.

The American decided he wasn't going to make the latter mistake and continued to scrutinize the ground as he headed for the airstrip.

Ricardo Figueroa finished speaking on the transmitter he carried, switched it off, and pushed its telescoping antenna into the body of the hand-held radio. He glanced at the bare light bulb that lit the tiny room reeking of sweat and turned to the knot of fourteen men half encircling him on the floor.

"Is it time?" one of the rebels asked anxiously.

Figueroa waited a moment to be sure he had everyone's attention. "The Yankee helicopter is headed back to the airstrip," he began, "just as our source said it would. So we must get to our positions. Remember, comrades, we'll try to hit the helicopter first while it's in the air. Then we'll smash through the perimeter and deal with the U.S. jet and the handful of Yankees guarding it with the weapons Zurita has given us. It's up to us now to strike this blow for all oppressed peoples." He surveyed the quiet faces around him and then stood at attention. "Death to the imperialists!"

"Death to the imperialists," the Shining Path guerrillas cried in unison, rising to their feet.

Father Ramero studied the Shining Path guerrillas as
they advanced along the hill toward the village, un-
knowingly aligning themselves with the hidden explosives. *Time to act,* the priest told himself. "Get down!"
he warned those along the stone fence beside him.
Concepcion Espinoza continued to fire over the top
of the bulwark. "Get down!" he yelled at her.

Finally when everyone along the wall was concealed, the cleric shoved the plunger of the blasting
machine.

Nothing happened.

"Holy Father," the priest hissed, lifting the blasting machine's plunger and shoving it again, more forc-
ibly this time to guarantee its generating enough
current to fire the blasting caps at the other end.

No explosion. As he checked the wires, a bullet
whined from the rock wall overhead, but the equipment seemed to be in order.

He tried again and still nothing happened.

He rose to inspect the wires running across the
wall and a slug smashed into a rock near his head.
"Stay down!" he warned those around him as he knelt

and reached into his robe to produce a stick of dynamite and the blue Bic lighter that Lloyd had given him.

The priest flicked on the lighter and held the flame to the fuse. As the detcord sputtered to life, he lobbed the dynamite stick over the barrier into the open area in front of him, then dropped behind the wall. "Keep down," he warned again.

Several seconds passed. Then a loud explosion signaled the priest's success as dust and rock came raining down.

Father Ramero peeked above the wall to see a few of the rebels struggling back to their feet, although the majority were lying motionless on the rocky ground. "There're still some left," he notified the villagers. "Someone give me a rifle."

He watched for a moment as his compatriots got into position and the snapping discharges of the .22 rifles filled the air.

A spare Marlin was passed down the line to the cleric. He worked the lever of the rifle, then lifted it to his shoulder, sighted, and snapped off a quick shot at one of the three remaining ruffians trying to flee.

Lloyd centered his sights on the last advancing rebel and squeezed the trigger. His carbine sent a single 32-grain bullet down the slope to smash into his adversary, and the man tumbled to the rocks and tobogganed along the incline.

As far as the geologist could tell, the machine gun Ernesto manned from the *punta* seemed to have demolished most of the rebels attacking from the eastern slope; there were no guerrillas to be seen. "Stay in your positions in case it's a trick," the American warned the villagers standing on either side of him, as they listened to the clatter of weapons from the other end of the village. "I'm going to see how the others are doing, so keep sharp."

Lloyd turned and sprinted across the open ground. Within minutes he had passed through the nearly empty village and was nearing its edge, when suddenly bullets ricochetted from the face of the hut next to him, whining angrily as the projectiles skipped along the face of the granite. He dropped to his knees, blinking in surprise as he searched for the sniper, but he saw nothing.

The machine gun on the *punta* above him clattered to life, firing a long burst at the unseen sniper. "Ernesto, I hope you're aiming more carefully than it sounds like," Lloyd muttered to himself as he rose.

Ammunition's going to be in seriously short supply if the rebel attack continues for long, the geologist thought to himself as he raced down the hill toward the west wall that encircled that part of the village; he stared past the stone barrier at the guerrillas charging the steep western slope. They saw him at the same moment, lifted their weapons, and expelled a furious salvo in his direction as he sprinted toward the comparative safety of the rock fence. As their bullets cracked by, he noticed a Shining Path machine gunner bring his SAW to bear on him.

Lloyd gritted his teeth, waiting for the inevitable impact of one or more of the projectiles as he prepared to devour the last few remaining yards. *Too late to turn back,* he thought, lowering his head and dashing forward, the bullets chipping rock and raising plumes of dust around him as he ran.

Finally he was behind the safety of the wall.

Lloyd groaned and let his breath escape, feeling sick at his stomach. He'd made it. It seemed impossible to him but he really was alive and unharmed.

He continued to gasp for breath as he glanced up and down along the wall. None of the villagers were firing at the rebels from this edge of the village. Most were simply cowering behind the granite, their faces glazed and their rifles clinched tightly in their hands. One nursed a minor wound; three knelt with eyes clamped shut, sobbing at the noisy guns approaching and the bullets impacting on the stone in front of them.

I've got to get these people to return the rebels' fire or we'll be overrun, Lloyd told himself. "Come on, get to your feet," he yelled. "You can't let them keep you pinned down or they'll kill us."

They looked over at him but made no effort to rise.

He decided to try a different tactic. "Orlando. Encalada. Encarnacion," he called to the nearest men. "Show your wives what it's like to be men instead of sniveling children!" At least maybe he could appeal to the macho pride of the villagers and force them to fight.

He didn't have time to see if anyone was going to do his bidding since he suddenly heard rebel footsteps nearing the fence. He leaped up and began firing over the wall, at first blindly and then, as the rebel bullets seemed to be falling wide of their mark, taking more careful aim. He tapped fast double shots with his M100 to send two hyper-velocity .22 slugs at each of his foes.

One of the rebel targets returned the American's fire. The burst of heavy AK bullets glanced off the stone next to the geologist, slashing his face and hand with chips of granite.

Instead of ducking, the American took a deep breath and fired three slugs at the guerrilla. The rebel clutched his throat and dropped like a rock. Lloyd glanced along the wall on either side of him. The villagers were now standing beside him, unleashing a withering salvo of projectiles at the few rebels struggling forward just ten yards away.

There was a frantic barrage from both sides and three of the villagers were downed by guerrilla bullets, but within seconds, the last of the revolutionaries had been cleared from the western ridge leading to Piton. At nearly the same instant, the machine gun on the *punta* above the village abruptly fell silent.

There was no sound other than the moaning of the wounded. The shooting had ceased.

"We've beaten them again," Lloyd whispered to himself. "We must have. It's so quiet."

Then he heard a distant pop and a soft whining sound that he hadn't heard since his days in the military. "Incoming," he yelled reflexively in English, recognizing immediately that the villagers didn't have any idea what his warning meant.

"Agachada rapida!" he shouted again, motioning with his hands as the mortar round dropped into the center of the village. The explosion decimated one of the huts, and bits of sharp rock came careening down

to earth, pelting the bewildered men and women surrounding Lloyd.

The American geologist tore through the village
as mortar rounds rained down from the sky. The air
had grown cold, and dark clouds blotted out the sun;
it seemed to Lloyd as if the end of the world might
well be at hand. *It* will *be the end of the world for us if
we don't stop that damned mortar,* he warned himself.

Another of the shells sang through the air, announcing its long, ballistic drop toward him. Gritting
his teeth, he wondered if he was about to die. The explosion ripped open the earth before him, pelting him
with rock, but he was not seriously injured. The geologist continued on across the village until he dropped
into the trench behind the town's northern wall, closest to the location from which the mortars seemed to
be originating.

"What is this weapon?" Father Ramero inquired.

"Mortars," Lloyd replied, lifting his binoculars
to inspect the valley and the hill opposite them.
"They're lobbing the rounds over that slope into the
village. They must have a spotter somewhere on the
hill, telling them if they're hitting us or not."

"I saw one of them by the bush to the east," the
priest pointed, even though Lloyd had his binoculars
glued to his face. "Yes, he's still there."

"Got him," Lloyd said. "He's our man. I wish—"

He was interrupted by another explosion, this
one close to the church. It was answered by a rumble
of thunder from the thick clouds moving in from the
mountains.

"I wish we had a rifle to pick him off with," Lloyd

said. "Our .22s aren't powerful enough. And the AKMs aren't accurate enough to hit the side of a barn." He lowered the binoculars and looked around. "Saluo," he called, spying the young messenger.

"Si, Senor Lloyd."

"Go to Ernesto and—if he's not out of ammunition—have him fire his machine gun at the man on the hill. See the man there by that bush?"

"Si."

"Have him shoot at that hombre. Hurry." The American watched the boy scamper away. Then he removed his binoculars and exchanged the magazine on his rifle for a full one. "Father, you take care of Maria if anything happens to me."

"You know I will," the cleric replied. "What are you going to do?"

"As soon as Ernesto starts shooting—"

Another explosive blast ripped through the village.

"—I'm going to run down the ravine," Lloyd continued, "then climb the hill and try to fire on the mortar crew." He slung his M100 across his back so it hung by its sling out of his way. "I'm hoping Ernesto will have hit the spotter by the time I start climbing the hill."

"Wait," Father Ramero began. "If some of us go with you, then—"

"There's no time; I'm going alone."

The priest opened his mouth to argue, his face lit by a lightning flash. But before he could say anything he was interrupted by Ernesto's machine gun, which had recommenced its loud thumping fire.

The slugs raised a cloud of dust near the distant rebel spotter.

"Just say a prayer for me," Lloyd yelled as he vaulted the granite fence and half ran, half stumbled down the ravine. There was another flash of lightning as a cold downpour soaked the American.

The rebel on the hill above Lloyd fired down at him, taking careful aim and making the rocks around the geologist come alive, dancing and jumping from the impacts of bullets. At the same instant, it felt to the American as if a hammer had struck his shoulder, nearly bowling him down the muddy hill.

He grabbed a bush with his other hand, holding himself up and quickly surveying his wound. He was startled to observe a gaping hole in the muscle of his shoulder, rapidly turning pink as the rain mixed with the blood oozing from it.

Lloyd again began to climb.

There was the distant popping of Ernesto's machine gun accompanied by a flash of lightning and an increase in the rain.

Lloyd was nearly dislodged from the face of the hill as a miniature avalanche of pebbles and mud slid toward him. The American looked upward to see the rebel spotter slide past, a large bullet hole weeping blood from his forehead.

Ernesto finally hit his mark, Lloyd thought grimly, climbing with renewed speed. "Way to go, Ernesto," he whispered, his breath rasping in his lungs as he neared the ridge.

At the top of the muddy hill, Lloyd unslung his weapon, aware of the stiffness in his arm. He thumbed off the safety of the Calico rifle, wondering why he hadn't had the sense to bring one of the more powerful AKMs with him before charging the hill. Attacking a mortar crew with a .22 rifle seemed insane.

It only seems that way because it is *insane,* Lloyd told himself. But he'd come too far to retreat. He took a deep breath and rose to charge over the ridge.

The rebel standing just on the other side of the hill gawked at the mud-covered, red-haired wildman that materialized in front of him. Thunder rolled across the hills as Lloyd swung his rifle toward the enemy and fired slugs as fast as his finger could pull the trigger.

The fat guerrilla was struck but wouldn't drop. Instead, he raised his own weapon, its safety making a loud click as he released it.

The American continued to fire, stitching the rebel's plump arms and chest. Finally a bullet punched into the man's throat, striking his backbone. He doubled up and skidded down the ridge, his spinal cord severed.

A second rebel sloshed up the hill toward Lloyd, firing recklessly, unsure if there were others with the American.

The guerrilla's flurry of shots went wide as he lost his footing on the muddy hillside; the bullets ricochetted harmlessly off the rocks several yards from Lloyd, who was taking careful aim. A single .22-caliber slug left the barrel of the M100 and almost instantly shredded the rebel's left eye, bringing an immediate halt to his counterattack.

The three guerrillas manning the mortar stared at the soaked giant silhouetted on the ridge by the lightning. The American opened fire, pumping the trigger of his rifle as rapidly as he could.

One of the rebels dropped immediately, grasping his chest. The other two came to life, moving quickly to avoid the attacker. One of the men shouldered his AKM to aim, then fell backward as if he'd been kicked by a bull, his finger squeezing the trigger as he fell, sending a wild stream of bullets skyward.

The third rebel was struck by one of the twenty-two caliber bullets and dropped the shell he'd been holding into the mortar. Only wounded, he tried to jump clear of the mortar tube as another of the American's bullets hit his knee.

The guerrilla toppled onto the mortar tube, horror spreading across his face. At that instant, the projectile erupted from the mouth of the mortar tube, exploding with a massive concussion that fired the twelve other mortars lying in the emplacement.

The massive blasts threw Lloyd onto his back, where he remained as a hail of gravel, bone, and flesh rained down on the area, mixing into the rain and mud. Another lightning flash lit the area and revealed the American lying motionless, the deep cuts in his forehead and neck bleeding profusely.

As the sun streamed through the helicopter ports, warming the cabin comfortably, Oz snapped off the heater module. The pilot was unsure how long this situation would continue, however, as he noticed an ominously black cloud headed their way from the Andes.

The TF/TA hauled them over yet another shantytown on their journey back to the Peruvian airbase; although the asymmetrical hamlet appeared to be one they'd flown over previously, they'd taken an alternate return route to prevent an ambush. The MH-60K rose over the rocky foothills towering beyond the village, skimmed a gentle peak, and then dropped in a giddy descent to the opposite side of the incline.

Oz checked the VSD, paying special attention to the terrain trace line at the base of the screen which showed the roller coaster ride still in store for them, the long, squiggly stripe corresponding to the rough topography ahead. Below the white traceline was a scale broken into kilometers, giving the precise location of each hill and valley ahead.

"I'm picking up Peruvian radar," Death Song informed the pilot. "We're about ten kilometers from the airstrip."

"Better get in touch for clearance," Oz responded. Since the Americans hadn't given the Peruvian military access to their interrogate-friend-or-foe codes, also known as IFF or "squawk," an accidental missile launch at the U.S. chopper could be disastrous since the rocket's electronic safeguards would be unable to identify them as "friendlies." While such an accident was unlikely, the Americans made it a practice to alert the Peruvians well ahead of time when they approached military installations.

The pilot switched to the Peruvian military frequency and triggered on his radio. "PNG-4, this is NS-1 requesting permission to land in our designated area. Over."

There was a hiss and then the answer came through in Spanish-accented English. "NS-1, you are granted permission to land in your designated area. Wind is from the east at four kph and we have a storm moving in from the northwest. What is your ETA please? Over."

"Our ETA is five minutes. Thanks, PNG-4. Over and out."

The chopper jumped another steep foothill as Oz clicked the radio to the U.S. air force frequency. "SP-Ground this is SP-1," he called on to the sergeant in charge of security at their destination. "Come in please. Over."

There was no answer. The pilot tried again. "SP-Ground this is SP-1, come in please. Over."

"SP-1," the voice of Sergeant Jason Quicke answered. "We read you loud and clear. Over."

"We're bringing our tired bones in within about three minutes," Oz said. "How's it look down there? Over."

"All's clear here. We'll be watching—hang on a sec. SP-1, it looks like something strange's going on."

The radio was silent for a moment before the air force security sergeant returned to the air, his voice slightly agitated. "SP-1, we have two unidentified trucks approaching us from three hundred yards south of the strip. Don't come in until we have a chance to check 'em out. Repeat, do *not* come in."

Quicke dropped off the air momentarily and then returned in a state of high excitement. "SP-1, we are under attack," he shouted, the sound of gunfire in the background. "Repeat, we are under attack. SP-Ground is signing off. Over and out."

Oz jerked reflexively at the control column and kicked the left rudder pedal, aborting their flight toward the landing strip, which was now only seconds away. "Death Song, arm our weapons. O.T. and Luger, man your guns."

"Weapons are armed," Death Song announced. "You've got the machine gun pod and rockets. I'll stand by with the Hellfires and countermeasures."

Oz lifted them at a low angle above the ridge approaching the airfield so they skimmed the earth. "Should be about—"

"Rocket launch!" Luger interrupted from the gunners cabin. "At five o'clock, coming in real fast."

Father Ramero gritted his teeth, trying not to shiver in the dampness. His muddy robe continued to flap against the back of his legs, feeling like a wet fish. *God must have a strange sense of humor,* the cleric reflected to himself. Normally the Lord sent less than an inch of rain each year; today he'd given them a whole year's worth of precipitation right in the middle of the battle. At least the cloudburst had almost stopped, except for an occasional droplet. The priest glanced toward the sky, still covered with inky clouds racing in the wind.

Ramero's thoughts returned to earth as he and the other men approached the rubble of one of the houses. "Be careful," the priest ordered the three as they helped him carry the inert body of the American geologist. "Don't bang his head against that rock! Remember, we're not carrying a bag of feed."

Ramero shook his head at the careless performance of the villagers, then he suddenly realized that most of them must still be in shock from the intense fighting they'd seen. Although only one of their number had been killed and seven others injured, they still had gazed into the Grim Reaper's eyes—many for the first time. He'd have to be easy on them until they'd recovered from the experience.

"Let's put him there," Ramero suggested to the men, pointing with his chin. "Over there on that table."

The four laborers scuttled toward the table like a giant, uncoordinated crab. The priest wondered absently what a table was doing in the middle of the muddy street. Then he realized someone had dragged it into the open in an attempt to salvage it from the wreckage of a nearby home destroyed by a mortar round.

"Lloyd!" Maria cried, splashing across the narrow street as the men placed the bloodied geologist's body on the table. The American lay motionless, his face deathly white.

"Father?" she demanded. "Is he dead?"

"No," Ramero responded, pushing a lock of wet, black hair out of his eyes. "His coloring is bad because he's lost some blood, but I don't think he's very seriously injured. We'll have the sister check him over him as soon as she's done with the others; she'll be able to tell. Here, sit by him. Hold his hand."

"Why is he unconscious if he isn't badly hurt?" she asked, laying her Ruger 10/22 next to her husband and sitting on a broken chair. "When will he awaken?"

"I don't know," Ramero replied, glancing at the sky again. It was starting to clear off and the sun seemed to be on the verge of breaking through the clouds. He looked at Maria. "I think the final blast of the mortars knocked him unconscious. But his cuts and the bullet hole in his shoulder—don't touch the bandage—are minor. He may have trouble hearing for a while—that was quite a blast, even from this side of the hill, but I think he'll be okay."

Suddenly, the sun broke through the clouds, spearing the village in a beam of light. The street was bathed in golden rays more intense than the priest could ever remember. As he studied Maria's face, he thought she had the aspect of a dark angel in the radiant sunlight.

"Look, Maria, he's stirring," the cleric said. As the woman stared down at her husband, his eyes fluttered open and he blinked a few times.

"Lloyd, are you all right?" she inquired anxiously.

The geologist closed his eyes again, blinked a few times, and when he reopened them, the most beatific smile slowly spread across his craggy features.

Why is Lloyd smiling like that? Ramero wondered, studying the broad grin on the geologist's face. *Has he lost his senses?*

The geologist seemed to be gawking at the *punta* towering behind the village. Ramero turned to scan the rise and found himself squinting into a brightness that was like looking into a blast furnace.

The cleric crossed himself. "Mother of God!" he whispered, fingering his crucifix. "Have mercy on us."

Raw sewage flowed through the narrow tunnel, choking Zurita despite the heavy cloth bandanna he'd tied across his mouth and nose. "How much farther?" he asked the scout, who had explored the passage before the plans had been finalized.

"Around that bend," Lopez replied, flicking the beam of his flashlight ahead to point the way. "We're almost there."

Zurita repositioned the heavy strap of the Redeye II that tore at his shoulder and tried not to retch. *Don't look at the water,* he warned himself. He'd made the mistake of glancing down at it once before and had nearly lost his breakfast.

It was like a journey into the bowels of hell. *Keep going,* he ordered himself. *You're the leader—act like it.*

They trudged on, flashlights pitifully dim in the gloomy darkness, heavily burdened with the shoulder-launched missiles and machines guns they'd taken from the government trucks Zurita had stolen.

"At least I have waterproof rubber boots," Zurita muttered to himself, his voice camouflaged by the roaring water that swirled in a stream alongside the ledge they walked on. Most of the thirty members in his party didn't even have that advantage; the thought of having the putrid water sloshing against his skin made him grip his AKM tighter, breathing through his mouth to prevent the stench from overpowering him.

Long minutes later, Lopez paused and flashed his light across the foul stream running between them and the concrete bank on the other side. The beam impaled a rusty ladder that led through a fissure in the concrete. "That's the tunnel we cut through the concrete during the night when the bank was empty. It leads into the sub-basement of the Transamerican Bank building," the guide explained.

"We have to cross the water?" Zurita asked, his voice echoing above the churning refuse.

"Si," the guide answered, stepping into the slurry.

"How deep is it?" Zurita inquired.

"Thigh deep in the middle," Lopez answered, wading into the deeper water, where shapes bobbed outside the beam of his flashlight.

Thigh deep! Zurita thought, gagging. The foul-smelling liquid would penetrate his clothing and fill his boots. He swallowed hard and turned to the men behind him. "Let's get going," he commanded, clenching his lips and splashing into the putrid, warm water, steeling himself for the ordeal.

One by one the thirty heavily laden Shining Path rebels crossed to the steel ladder. Within minutes, they scrambled up the ladder and through the rough hole. They entered a humming, hissing maze of heating ducts, plastic pipes, and wiring that fed upward into the Transamerican Bank building above.

"We can get to the stairs from the far end of this corridor," Lopez whispered to Zurita. "They lead clear to the roof."

The leader consulted his glow-in-the-dark watch. "We're behind schedule," he declared, turning to the guerrilla who carried the explosives. "Get the dynamite charges ready so we can seal off the stairs behind us, but don't cut it too close with the timer. It's better to be late than to alert the guards before we get into position—or blow ourselves up."

Zurita then turned back to address Lopez. "Lead the way. If we encounter anybody, we'll need to silence them immediately."

"I'll handle it," Lopez promised, drawing a fifteen-inch machete from the scabbard slung across his back. The stained blade's sharpened edge shimmered in the dim light.

The rebel band crept through the darkness up to the stairwell, leaving a trail of water and sludge behind that made it look as if a giant slug had crawled through the sub-basement complex.

8

"Bank left! Bank left!" O.T. warned from his position in the gunner's window.

Oz threw the MH-60K into a tight turn, skimming along the rise to present a minimal target to the rocket that chased them.

"It's guided," O.T. called. "It's turning after us."

Death Song activated the 532 countermeasure dispenser pod, and a stream of chaff erupted from the system, swirling behind them to reflect any radar beams that might be in use to direct the missile. Another tap on the console of the countermeasures controls launched an infrared flare which sputtered on its parachute to be swept along in the wake of the helicopter; the IR jammer aft of the main rotor came to life at the same instant, creating an intermittent pattern designed to confuse the electronics of an incoming heat-seeking warhead.

The oncoming missile ignored the cloud of chaff, gaining on the aircraft.

"It's still got us!" Luger warned, hanging tightly onto his Minigun's mounting ring as Oz jerked the control column to throw the helicopter down a steep ridge. "Wait, it's chasing the flare!" Luger shouted before losing sight of the oncoming rocket behind the rise.

There was an explosion and then a fireball rolled above the ridge.

"Must be heat-seeking," Death Song remarked.

"SP-1, this is SP-Ground, come in please," the voice of Sergeant Quicke erupted from the radio.

"This is SP-1, what's going on?" Oz replied.

"We've got two trucks outside the fence," the soldier answered. "They've got us pinned down with machine guns, but we've stopped them with our M60s—had 'em loaded with SLAPs and we shot out their tires and engines. But they're armed to the teeth and we're running out of ammunition."

"I'll circle around and try to get the trucks," Oz responded, swinging the chopper toward the ridge.

"Be careful, they have rockets," Quicke cautioned. "They've already downed several Peruvian choppers."

"We've found that out the hard way," Oz replied. "They seem to be infrared homers, if you want to pass that along to the Peruvians. Over and out." Oz released the radio and spoke into the intercom. "Everybody get ready. We're going in low."

The American MH-60K tore across the ridge, targeted by a .50-caliber machine gun mounted on the nearest of two military trucks next to the airstrip. The volley cut into the rotors and thumped against the metal skin of the helicopter, activating the metal fragment warning lights on the panel in front of Oz.

"SP-Ground," Oz radioed the air force security

sergeant, "the Peruvians in the military trucks are firing at us!"

"Negative, negative, SP-1," Quicke yelled. "Those are *not* Peruvian military. They *are* your targets. Over."

Oz didn't need anymore assurance. He dropped the chopper lower to skim the sand and rocks, aligning the nose of the helicopter with the closest truck, and then tapped the rocket launch button on the control column. Two 70mm rockets coughed out of their pod, their wings springing out and rockets flaring to life in a blur of speed.

The Hydra 70 rockets ripped into the truck ahead of Oz as he lifted the chopper out of the cloud of smoke and debris which the downward blast of the rotors churned into black swirls.

The second truck's gunner trained his machine gun on the American chopper as they passed, its tracer bullets etching red lines to the left of Oz.

"Another rocket at eight o'clock," O.T. yelled above the whining thunder of his GE M134 Minigun. The spinning barrels discharged, the mechanism of the weapon automatically yanking ammunition from a four-thousand round linked belt.

"I'm banking hard right," Oz warned his crew, shoving the control column to starboard and kicking the right pedal to alter their course away from the oncoming missile.

Death Song released another flare.

"It's going after the flare," O.T. announced.

"I see the guys with the rockets," Luger yelled. "They're in the clump of bushes south of the airstrip."

He aimed his Minigun carefully and pulled the trigger.

Long flames gushed out of its six barrels, sending a swarm of .30-caliber slugs at the knot of men hidden among the boulders on the ridge. Luger watched as the rebels dropped into the sand, while several of the warheads on the rockets exploded nearby.

Oz dropped into another attack run toward the remaining truck whose gunner was again concentrating his fire on the approaching helicopter. The pilot shoved the control column forward for greater speed as a stream of tracers leaped from the truck and raced past the cabin. Oz altered his course slightly, then hit the red button on the control column to send three more rockets from their pod. The missiles hissed from their tubes and raced toward the vehicle.

The first rocket struck the airstrip beyond the truck, generating a geyser of sand and rock. The second hit the cab, blowing it apart and bringing an immediate cessation to the machine gun fire. The third missile smashed into the fuel tank, creating a giant fireball ahead of the chopper, threatening to engulf it in flame.

Oz jerked on the collective pitch lever and threw the column to the side in an effort to elude the fireball they were rushing toward. The chopper tore upward, throwing the four crew members backward into their seats.

The flames lapped at the helicopter's hull as both continued to climb, but the chopper finally broke through the smoke and bolted skyward.

"Is everybody okay back there?" Oz barked, alarmed at the possibility that his two gunners might have been burned by the flames coming through their open windows.

"A little medium-rare but okay," O.T. cracked.

"I see a band of men at three o'clock," Luger announced. "They're rushing the fence next to the transport."

Oz wheeled the chopper about and aligned the nose of the aircraft with the remaining squad of guerrillas advancing toward the fence of the airfield below.

"Here they come!" the air force private warned, surveying the guerrillas charging the fence.

"Sarge, I'm down to one magazine," one of the team members called.

"Screw the ammo, get the guy with the dynamite!" Sergeant Quicke roared above the din of the M60 next to him.

The rebels dashed forward, generating such a heavy salvo that Quicke found it impossible to aim. Their bullets ricocheted from the runway and tore holes in the hangar shielding the Americans.

An air force rifleman cried out and fell, a large flower of blood blossoming on his uniform. A second turned toward Quicke, his rifle empty; before he could speak, his face exploded as a bullet caught him in the crown of the head.

Sergeant Quicke wiped the soldier's blood out of his eyes, ignoring the hail of small-arms bullets pattering against the skin of the hangar. He knew he had to concentrate on hitting the rebel charging the fence with the sticks of dynamite, their short fuses sizzling.

If that bastard makes it through the fence, he'll destroy the transport for sure, Quicke realized, glancing at the jet parked a hundred yards from the fence of the tiny airstrip. He sighted carefully and pulled the M16's trigger.

Nothing happened.

Quicke swore loudly and checked the side of the receiver. The bolt was locked rearward, indicating an empty magazine. He dropped the rifle and drew his pistol out of its hip holster.

At the same moment, the M60 sputtered to a stop. "I'm out of ammo, Sarge," the gunner yelled.

Shit! Quicke said to himself, drawing a bead with his M9 pistol on the rebels cutting through the fence, the heavy barrage of RPKs making it just a matter of time before he was hit.

Quicke pumped the trigger of his pistol rapidly, hitting the guerrilla with the wire cutters. His last bullet struck the rebel carrying the dynamite, but the man was only wounded in the leg.

The insurgent stumbled, then regained his balance and pushed his way through the hole in the fence. He hobbled several yards, then prepared to hurl the explosives toward the hangar where Quicke stood watching helplessly with his empty Beretta.

Oz slowed the chopper, kicking a pedal to align the aircraft with the clump of men standing at the fence.

As they approached the enemy, O.T. punched a long string of bullets from his Minigun, aiming at a second group of guerrillas that had split away from the first party to storm another section of the fence. The muzzles of the Gatling-like weapon sent a fusillade earthward that slashed into the men, cutting down all eight of them.

Oz hit the fire button on the control column, adjusting his path to walk the plumes of dirt kicked up by his bullets into the clump of men climbing through the fence. The twin .30-caliber machine guns in the starboard pod continued to blaze away as the pilot threw the chopper into a "tree topper," circling the guerrillas on the ground while the nose of the chopper remained on target.

When he had hit the last three rebels, Oz slammed the control column forward, nosing the chopper down and leaving the area at maximum speed to avoid an attack by enemy rockets. Seconds after the MH-60K passed over the dead guerrillas, a massive explosion thundered behind it.

"What the hell was that?" Oz called over the intercom.

"I'm not sure," Luger answered. "Looks like one of the rebels we hit dropped a satchel charge or something. Blew one mother of a hole in the edge of the tarmac."

"Anybody see any other guerrillas?" Oz asked.

"Negative on the port side," O.T. responded after scanning the ground.

"I think that's all on the starboard," Luger agreed, leaning from his window to double check.

Oz circled the airstrip once more, noting two burning Peruvian UH-1H Iroquois in flames at the far edge of the field.

"SP-Ground, this is SP-1, can you read me?"

"Got ya, SP-1. Thanks for saving our bacon,"

Quicke responded. "That guy had seven sticks of dynamite."

"We were wondering what the explosion was. We're coming in if it looks like the rebels are down. We don't see any from here."

"It's clear here, too," Quicke replied.

"Have you contacted our care package?" Oz asked. "I'm betting this is an isolated attack. But if it's part of a concerted plan—"

"I'm reading you, SP-1. I'll get in touch with them right away. Over and out."

9

Lloyd rose to his elbows, mesmerized like a moth circling a bright flame. He gazed into the sunlight reflecting off the *punta,* his ears ringing from the explosion; he was only vaguely aware of the babble of villagers' voices as they encircled him.

Maria assisted him to his feet and helped escort him as he staggered toward the light. He stumbled once, then draped his arms over the shoulders of Father Ramero and his wife. The villagers collecting around the three grew strangely silent and formed a procession toward the tall horn of rock that shone like a lighthouse at the rear of the village, its beacon of sunlight drawing them to it.

The procession ended at the base of the *punta,* where the American geologist gazed upward at the smooth, mirror-like surface ten feet above the ground. "I can't believe it," he whispered, taking another faltering step toward it. He reached out and tentatively established a handhold within a crevice. As his strength began to return gradually with the pumping of adrenaline through his veins, he climbed up on shaky legs and arms until he had reached the mineral deposit that reflected the sunlight so brightly it made his eyes ache.

He could feel the warm sunlight as it reflected from the golden surface onto his face. Stretching out his hand, he ran his palm across its cool smoothness to be sure what he saw was real.

The villagers stood in awe below, the priest continuing to clutch his crucifix as he gaped at the American geologist, transfigured by the bright, golden mirror.

Lloyd broke the reverent silence. "It's the mother lode we've been searching for!" he bellowed. "It's been right here all the time!"

Heedless of his well being, the geologist jumped off his high perch, landing in a tangle of arms and legs below to be raised to his feet by the townspeople, who now cheered and wept and laughed, pushing forward to get a closer look at the huge outcropping of gold.

"A mortar round must have blown away the granite matrix hiding it," Lloyd said to no one in particular. Although he could hear the shouting next to him, he was still unable to discern what anyone was saying. "It's almost pure," he said to Father Ramero, who was scowling. "Only a little electrum mixed in with it—and only at the edges. Mostly, it's undiluted. I can't believe—"

The villagers hoisted the American to their shoulders and carried him, still half deaf, like a saint through the muddy streets of Piton at the beginning of what was to be a huge, impromptu celebration.

The meeting between Vice-President Decker and Peruvian President Esteban was conducted on the top floor of the Transamerican Bank building. The site had been selected to keep the meetings businesslike and to force everyone to get to the subjects on the agenda without wasting time on protocol or ceremony.

Two sides of the room were expanses of smoked glass, giving a panoramic view of Lima, its nearby buildings glistening impressively. The other walls were decorated with brightly painted murals. Roses in huge, earthen urns filled the air with their thick fragrance, while recessed spotlights splashed intense beams of illumination across the conference members.

Vice-President Decker noticed the momentarily stunned look on Bishop's face when a janitor stepped out of a concealed lavatory whose door was part of the mural. There was no doubt that Bishop knew about the lavatory—he'd probably memorized the plans to the building—but the vice-president could see the surprise on the agent's face when the janitor appeared.

Bishop glanced toward one of his men. *Bet the SOB's going to chew one of his men out for not letting him know about the janitor,* the vice-president thought, smiling to himself.

The agent motioned and the janitor was hastily escorted from the room. There was no doubt in Decker's mind that Bishop was good, but the vice-president found him a royal pain in the butt, and it made him feel good to see the agent make a mistake.

The American dignitary settled into his chair on one side of the long, glass-topped table and studied the murals of the Spanish shaking hands with the Incas. *Not the way I remember Peruvian history,* he thought grimly. He remembered how his college history prof had put it. "First the Spanish fell on their knees, then they fell on the aborigines."

The vice-president glanced toward his two staff members and the diplomats from the nearby American embassy who flanked him. He started to take a drink of water from the glass in front of him, then thought better of it lest he start the meeting by spilling the liquid. What the press wrote about his clumsiness wasn't entirely false, and he didn't care to do anything to bolster his reputation in that regard.

The Peruvians gradually became quiet.

Decker cleared his throat and began to speak. "On behalf of the government of the United States, I wish to thank the government of Peru for inviting us here today. As you undoubtedly know—"

An explosion in the corridor outside brought his speech to an abrupt halt as everyone in the room jumped to his feet.

Oz brought the chopper in at a shallow approach for a running landing on the smooth airstrip. This would allow the craft to touch down quickly while avoiding a hover, which would make them an easy target if the enemy were still in the area.

"Get Bishop on the radio," Oz told Death Song.

The pilot approached the airfield, carefully keeping the chopper on course through coordinated movements on the collective pitch lever to lower the aircraft, while simultaneously maintaining his heading by increasing pressure on the right rudder pedal and retaining the airspeed with the control column. When he was fifty feet over the airfield, he gradually pulled on the control column to lower their airspeed. At the same time, he lowered the collective pitch lever to touch the chopper to the earth and smoothly made a rolling stop on the concrete surface. He pushed down on the collective pitch lever to anchor them to the earth, then throttled down the engine.

"Captain," Death Song said, "I can't seem to get in touch with Bishop. I guess he isn't answering his radio—or maybe he's having radio trouble."

"If he's having radio trouble he'll be getting in touch with the base by phone," Oz told his copilot. "Bishop's no-nonsense." He thought a second. "Let's contact the Peruvian military and see what they've got. I can't imagine anyone being able to get into the Transamerican building without a full-scale military operation. That place looked like a fortress with the barricades and machine-gun nests they have surrounding it, but we'd better find out what's going on there just in case."

Oz spoke to his gunners. "O.T. and Luger, see if you can locate our ground crew. Let's get the missile pod refilled from the stores we brought. And pick up more belts for our machine guns."

"Will do, captain," O.T. replied, unbuckling his harness. "Come on, Luger, I think that's the ground crew coming toward us."

"Death Song," the pilot said, "I'm going outside to check the copter and to be sure it didn't sustain any serious damage. In the meantime, contact Commander Warner via COMSAT and apprise him of what's happened."

"Yes, sir."

Oz unfastened his harness, removed his helmet,

and vaulted out of the chopper to pace alongside the olive green MH-60K, examining its exterior closely for signs of damage. There were a number of .50-caliber hits scoring its skin and a widely spaced line of bullet pocks crossing the drive shaft cover. The pilot was thankful for the chopper's substantial armor. *If we'd been hit like this flying a Huey,* he realized, *we'd have gone down for sure.*

Crossing to the front of the machine, he noticed the lower spall-resistant chin window on Death Song's side had also taken a hit from a rifle; a .30-caliber bullet was encased in the Plexiglass like a fly in amber.

The port side of the MH-60K was nearly unmarked except for three grooves indicating spots where bullets had streaked along the skin at an extreme angle, ricochetting harmlessly off the chopper. The metal skin was also coated with black soot from the fireball they'd skirted.

Everything appeared sound on the exterior of the twenty-five-thousand-pound fighting machine. And Oz was confident, with its redundant hydraulic and electrical systems, that the chopper would be able to operate without incident if they had to take to the air any time soon.

"Captain, I've informed the commander of our situation," Death Song called through the side window of the aircraft. "He'd like to speak to you ASAP."

"I'll be right there," the pilot answered, striding to his door and unlatching it. He stepped onto the rung jutting from the fairing of the port landing gear and slung himself into the cockpit. After slipping on his helmet and centering the mike over his mouth, he toggled on the radio. "Mother Hen, this is SP-1, over."

"SP-1," Warner's voice answered, "is everything under control there? Over."

"Yes, but it looks like our air force security team has sustained a few casualties from the looks of it—I haven't had a chance to speak to Sergeant Quicke yet so I don't have any numbers. And at least two Peruvian choppers are destroyed; I can see the wreckage from here. Over."

"Death Song mentioned rockets."

"Yeah. Our attackers had shoulder-launched heat seekers and plenty of explosives and small arms, too. Over."

"We have a report from the Peruvians that two *Guardia Republicana* trucks carrying a shipment of LAW-80s and Redeye IIs were hijacked late yesterday, so you need to keep a very sharp lookout for rockets. Have you had radio contact with the dogs you dropped at your previous LZ?"

"That's a negative, Mother Hen. Our security sergeant's working on that right now. Over."

"Our embassy reports that they've lost contact with the meeting from their end, so it sounds like we may have more trouble, but it's hard to tell—communications and power facilities are always under attack from the rebels. Just the same, I'd like for you to return to your previous LZ just to be on the safe side. Is your chopper up to that? Over."

"Yes, I just checked it. We're getting our weapons replenished and will be ready shortly. I'd say our ETA at the LZ should be twenty minutes. Over."

"Good. I'll check into the situation and let you know as soon as we uncover anything. Over."

"I'll contact you right before we arrive if that's okay. Over."

"Sounds good. Over and out."

10

Bishop covered the double doors of the stairwell with his TEC-9K, its electroless-nickel finish gleaming in the dim light. The corridor was only faintly lit by emergency lights since the power had failed with the explosion.

The doors swung open.

The agent raised the muzzle of his weapon, no longer covering agent Raborn, who'd pushed his way into the corridor.

"What the hell was that!" Bishop yelled.

Raborn coughed. "An explosion, sir."

"I know that! What exploded?"

The agent ran a hand through his hair, stiff with concrete dust. "I think they've destroyed the stairs. I heard someone in the stairwell and checked—and then the explosion. I glanced down right afterward when the emergency lights came on and it looked like at least two flights were missing. But its hard to tell with the smoke and dust. Shall I check the roof?"

"No," Bishop answered glancing at the elevators. "Let's secure this floor first."

Both elevators had stopped at the roof and appeared to be functioning on emergency power as well. Bishop crossed over to them quickly and punched the down button, taking care to keep the muzzle of his TEC-9K pointed in a safe direction. He turned back to Raborn. "Keep track of the elevators. Be sure there're friendlies on the first one that comes down. Then block the elevator door open so it'll be here if we need it. Let the other one go after you've verified there are no terrorists in it so the soldiers below us can ride it back up."

"Yes, sir."

"Williams," Bishop called to another of the agents who guarded the conference room door, along with four nervous Peruvian soldiers.

"Yes, sir," Williams answered.

"Get to the end of the hall and watch for anybody that doesn't belong up here. If you see anybody, shoot 'em. We'll have time for genteel conversations later."

"Yes, sir."

"Lawrence," Bishop called to one of the two agents holding Colt Commandos inside the conference room. "Find out what that shooting's about on the roof and the other buildings."

"Yes, sir."

Bishop turned back to the elevators, both of which were still on the roof. "Damn," he erupted. He knelt by his briefcase, which he'd dropped to extract his TEC-9K, and rapidly procured two stun grenades and hooked them into his belt. He had just removed his radio to call Captain Carson, when Lawrence came running toward him.

"Sir, whoever's above us on the roof is shooting

at the machine gun emplacements on the other buildings."

"Shit! Looks like we're trapped here until the Peruvians can root them off the roof!" Bishop exclaimed angrily, turning to the agents and soldiers standing in the hallway. "Okay, you guys. You need to watch the stairs and the elevators. There's no telling who'll be coming down. Williams, keep the dignitaries in the conference room. Better yet, get them crowded into the washroom—it has solid concrete walls."

"Yes, sir."

Bishop crossed to the double doors leading to the stairs and shoved his way through to stand on the landing, trying not to cough in the thick cement dust floating in the air. He leaned over the railing and stared upward.

A shot echoed down the stairwell seconds after Bishop had jerked his head back. *That settles who's up there,* he realized, pushing back through the double doors and re-entering the corridor. "They have the roof," he announced, "but the Peruvian military choppers should be able to take them out in short order *if* we can keep them up there."

"The vice-president and the Peruvians are in a chamber off the conference room," Williams reported, coming back into the corridor.

"Good," Bishop responded. "I'm betting these guys will be coming down the stairs or elevators any minute. We're going to have to be ready for them."

The agent again took his radio from its belt pouch when both elevators suddenly departed from the roof.

"Sir!" Williams yelled, pointing toward the elevators.

"I see it. Everybody over here!" Bishop hollered to the agents and the Peruvian guards. "Get down. You, get to the side. Shoot anyone holding a gun."

As first one and then the other elevator arrived, the guards and secret service agents raised their weapons.

The doors cracked open.

Before the elevators had completely revealed the six riders in each car, the soldiers and agents fired. The muzzle flashes lit the darkened corridor, and empty brass cartridges rang across the marble floor, spewing from the ejection ports of the Uzis, TEC-9K, and AKMs.

The storm of bullets riddled the rebels who returned the fusillade, spraying wildly through the opening doors.

The gunfire stopped as abruptly as it had begun when those in the hallway had exhausted the ammunition in their magazines. The guerrillas lay in a heap inside the perforated elevator cars.

Though the bloody fight had lasted merely three seconds, hundreds of rounds had been expended, polluting the air in the hallway with the acrid fumes of burnt gunpowder.

Bishop dropped the empty magazine from his machine pistol, retrieved a full magazine from the special harness under his jacket, and slapped it into place with a loud click. Then he jerked the charging handle and released it. He kept the dead men in the elevators covered for a few more seconds and then, satisfied none posed any danger, glanced down the corridor.

Two of the Peruvian soldiers, along with Williams and Lawrence, remained standing. A wounded trooper lying on the floor began to moan, holding his bloody chest. The other men on the floor—three agents and four soldiers—had been killed by the rebels' salvo.

"Williams, you and the soldiers watch the stairwell," Bishop ordered. "They'll be coming down the stairs next. Lawrence, get that soldier's first-aid pouch open and cover his chest wound."

The agent and troops stationed themselves by the double doors leading to the stairs. Bishop made his way toward the elevators and pulled a body from each halfway into the hall to block the sliding doors and lock the elevators in place. *We could head down in the elevators if we knew there weren't rebels on the floor below,* he thought as he worked. *But if there are, they could fire through the doors when we pass—with the same consequences as the men in these cars experienced.* They'd better stay put until the cavalry came to rescue them, he decided.

"Speaking of which," Bishop muttered, reaching for his radio a third time. The agent pulled the transmitter from his belt and held it for a second, then threw it away with a loud oath. A bullet had pierced its body, shattering the electronics inside.

A rebel moaned and stirred when Bishop stepped out of the elevator. The secret service agent whirled around and covered the man.

The guerrilla rose to his elbows, his eyes open.

Bishop tapped the trigger of his weapon and fired a single round. The bullet crashed into the insurgent's skull, killing the man instantly. *No time for prisoners,* the agent told himself, turning away.

"I can hear someone talking at the top of the stairs," Williams whispered.

"Come down this hallway," Bishop directed the soldiers and two remaining agents. *Time for round two,* he thought grimly.

Zurita and his band of rebels had little trouble getting to the roof and taking the lax guards there, but all else had not gone smoothly. The worst of it was that the dynamite charge the guerrillas left on the stairway exploded prematurely, warning the Americans and Peruvians that something was amiss. That, Zurita was sure, had given the capitalists the warning they needed to slaughter the men he'd sent down in the pair of elevators.

Now Lopez was preparing to aim an LAW-80 at the last remaining machine gun nest on the roof of a nearby building. The soldiers manning the gun fired toward the northern edge of the Transamerican Bank roof, leaving Lopez open to lean over the guard rail and carefully align the striata lines on the soldiers.

He smashed the launch lever atop the tube that rested on his shoulder and the rocket jumped from the launcher, the backwash of its jets warming his scalp. The blast carried the missile into the space between the buildings where the booster engine kicked in, accelerating the projectile toward its target.

The warhead struck the sandbags and exploded

in front of the Peruvian soldiers manning the .30-caliber FN MAG T14 machine gun, peppering the men with metal fragments and hurling the tripod-mounted gun onto its side.

Zurita eyed the smoldering machine gun nest across the street and slapped Lopez on the shoulder. "Good work," he congratulated. "Now keep a sharp lookout for government snipers or helicopter gunships. I'm betting they'll try to land a chopper here next. I'm putting you in charge of handling the Redeyes."

Lopez threw the empty launcher down and lifted another LAW-80, extending its tube so it would be ready to be fired at a moment's notice. "We'll take care of anyone up here," he vowed to Zurita.

Crossing to the stairwell leading to the floor below, Zurita stopped by another group of his men as they prepared to storm the stairs leading to the top floor. "Ready?" he asked.

They murmured agreement, though not too enthusiastically, Zurita noted, since they had already watched twelve of their comrades descend in the elevators and fail to return.

"Remember, we have the capitalist oppressors cut off," Zurita reassured them. "Without reinforcements, they're nothing. We've destroyed the stairs below them and now we have the power to the elevators cut off. Most of the soldiers and American bodyguards were probably killed during our first attack."

"Perhaps you'd like to lead us then?" muttered one of the men in the group.

"I'm going to do just that, Comrade Aguilar," Zurita responded, glaring at the troublemaker. "Do *you* have the *machismo* to attack a handful of capitalists with me, little brother?"

Aguilar didn't answer.

Zurita addressed the others. "Be sure the selectors on your rifles are set to full auto and you have a round in the chamber," he told them, waiting as they checked their AKMs. Then he continued. "Remember, we want the president and the Yankee vice-president alive; kill the others if you have to, but we must take those two alive."

"We will prevail, Comrade Zurita," Aguilar promised, trying to regain his leader's favor.

Zurita paused, inhaled deeply, and then whooped a deafening war cry as he jumped through the open doors, his men pouring down the stairs behind him.

"I'd like to send you in now," Warner radioed to Oz as the American pilot approached Lima, "but the Peruvians have requested that you hang back until they get their helicopters onto the roof. They're also working on getting a team up the stairwell—three-and-a-half flights were demolished by dynamite and the rebels left behind a bunch of booby traps—it's going to take a while."

"Are our people safe?" Oz asked.

"There's no way to know since we don't have phone or radio communication with them," Warner answered. "There've been a lot of reports of shooting there and the rebels now have control of the area, thanks to their higher vantage point. Over."

"Can't the government troops blast them off the roof from the nearby buildings?"

"The rebels have the high ground in the area and have taken advantage of the rockets they stole to severely damage the buildings the Peruvians are trying to operate from. And the government doesn't want to counter with rockets if they can keep from it—at least not until they've evacuated everyone from the area. Over."

"What do the guerrillas want?"

"No demands yet. That suggests some of the officials may still be safe. But even so, they're still cut off from the soldiers that were supposed to be protecting them."

"I don't see how they can hold out for long," Oz said.

"It looks like the rebels had at least thirty men, according to observers on the adjoining roofs," Warner reported. "We only had eight secret service agents, and the Peruvians think there were five additional soldiers on the floor when the stairs were demolished. Given the element of surprise, I doubt that all our people survived. Over."

"Do the Peruvians know that the rebels have Redeye IIs?" Oz asked.

"Yes, but I'm afraid they don't realize how much more effective the new models are," Warner said. "The joker I talked to didn't understand that the missiles could be launched head on rather than only chasing hot exhaust trails like the originals, and he didn't want to be told, either."

"So they'll be lucky if they don't lose additional aircraft taking the roof," Oz said.

"That's right."

"We'll stay out of the way and keep our fingers crossed," Oz said, reducing the chopper's speed.

"Keep me apprised of the situation," Warner ordered. "Over and out."

Oz threw the control column to the left and kicked a rudder pedal to circle the Transamerican Bank from a safe distance. It was almost noon and the overhead sun threw the chopper's shadow almost directly below them, where it jumped the avenues and buildings the MH-60K overflew.

Oz's radio again came to life. "NS-1 this is Peruvian BY-14," the pilot of the UH-1H called. "We're ahead of you at one o'clock. Come in, please."

"We see you, BY-14," Oz acknowledged. "We'll be hanging back out of your way. Over."

"Thanks, NS-1. You can follow us in after we kill the vermin."

"Sounds good to me," Oz said. "We discovered the hard way they have heat-seeking missiles. Over."

"Just some anti-tank weapons and a few Red-eyes," the pilot responded. "I'm betting we'll shake those and have our leaders out of the trap in a couple of minutes. Talk to you later. Over and out."

I hope they know what they're doing, Oz thought to himself, switching off the transmitter.

He had a terrible feeling they didn't.

As the guerrillas burst through the double doors of the stairwell, AKMs blazing, they riddled the walls and hammered the dead bodies that lay in the hallway.

There was no return fire.

"Stop shooting!" Zurita shouted. "No one's here."

The men regrouped around the door, covering the darkened corridor with the muzzles of their AKMs.

"Perhaps the Yankees are playing hide and seek," Aguilar suggested, squinting into the near darkness.

"So it seems," Zurita replied quietly. Before he could continue, muzzle flashes cut through the darkness at the end of the hallway, creating a thunderous din.

As Aguilar clutched his chest and stumbled, Zurita whirled and triggered a long burst from his AKM, his tracers inscribing red lines in the darkness. He fired from the hip, adjusting the hosing action of his bullets to converge on one and then another of the flashes that confronted him in the darkness.

A bullet cracked past his head and another smashed into his forearm as the Maoist extracted a full magazine from his harness and expertly exchanged it for the empty one, ignoring his wound. He straightened up and fired, this time in short bursts to hit the enemy by aiming at their muzzle flashes. He paced forward as he shot, advancing on the Americans and Peruvians who hadn't yet been hit by his compatriots' heavy barrage.

The firing from the corridor ahead abruptly ceased.

Zurita dropped to one knee and squinted into the darkness, suspecting the enemy had again hidden themselves, although his comrades continued their volley. "Hold your fire," he yelled.

Except for the soft moans of the wounded, the hallway was instantly silent. Zurita glanced behind him and saw that six of his men were still standing. "Get down and reload," he ordered. Allowing his rifle to hang on his shoulder by its sling, he drew an RPN offensive hand grenade from under his poncho. Glancing to either side to confirm that his men were crouching, he jerked the arming pin and hurled the grenade along the floor toward the darkness at the end of the hallway.

As the grenade rolled toward its destination, the rebel leader dropped to one knee.

Three seconds later, it exploded, its aluminum shrapnel stitching the walls around it; several of the low-density fragments harmlessly bounced off the paneling next to Zurita, their momentum reduced by air resistance.

"Come on," Zurita ordered, his rifle in hand. The guerrillas charged down the hall, meeting with no resistance this time. As their leader held up his hand, the rebels stopped beside three bodies—one American agent and two Peruvian soldiers—lying on the floor.

Zurita glanced around the corner.

The passageway was empty.

As he peered down the intersecting hallway again, he decided what to do next. "The conference room is around this corner," he whispered to the others. "When we get to it, we'll toss two grenades in. We'll follow them in after they explode." He drew another grenade from his pouch. "Cesar, you help with the other one."

The rebel leader rose with his men and charged down the hallway toward the large carved doors. As he and Cesar pulled the pins on their RPN grenades,

Zurita placed his shoulder against one of the doors, cracked it open, and ordered, "On three!"

The rebel leader drew a breath and counted, "One, two, *three!*"

The two hurled the grenades inside, then leaped aside to be clear of the doors should anyone fire through them. The grenades exploded, shaking the interior of the conference room.

Moments later, Zurita shoved through the doors, holding his gun at the ready. Except for the rebels, the room was empty.

The revolutionary swore vehemently in Spanish. He had expected the Americans to fight to the death; instead they were hiding like children. Their hide-and-seek strategy was consuming valuable time—something the guerrillas were short on since they needed the two officials for bargaining chips.

"Cesar!" Zurita demanded, turning to the rebel.

"Yes, comrade."

"Go to the roof and get everyone but Lopez and whoever's assisting him with the rockets. We're going to have to search the entire floor. And hurry up! We're running out of time."

Cesar nodded and left.

Zurita surveyed the rest of his men. "Spread out and search this floor," he commanded. "Keep a close lookout for the capitalists—they're here somewhere. Be careful of another ambush."

In the tiny lavatory off the conference room, the American and Peruvian delegates held their breaths, wondering if the rebels had noticed the half-hidden entrance to their hiding place.

Bishop grasped his TEC-9K tightly, watching

through the keyhole; the rebels were leaving but he had no doubt they'd return soon. The agent straightened up and studied the tiny window that allowed a small amount of sunlight to filter into the lavatory. He suddenly realized there might be an escape from the trap they'd fallen into.

Using a lightweight Spyderco pocketknife that he flicked open with his thumb, he rapidly pried the rubber seals off the window. Once the pane came loose, he carefully extracted it with the edge of the knife and carried it to the sink. Then he grasped the mirror above the marble sink, ripping it from its fasteners, and carried it to the narrow window.

With any luck, this just might work, Bishop thought, lifting the mirror.

C H A P T E R

12

The side windows of the Peruvian UH-1H Iroquois helicopters flashed in the sunlight as they wheeled into formation and streaked toward the Transamerican Bank building, weaving among the concrete structures of the city to remain hidden from the rebels until the last possible moment. The lead chopper boasted four side-mounted 7.62mm machine guns; the rear helicopter sported dual 12-rocket packs on its sides.

Each UH-1H carried a twelve-man team of *Cinchis*, highly trained anti-guerilla strike forces; the elite troops toted short-barreled AKR submachine guns chambered for the Soviet 5.45mmx39 cartridge; silenced PB Makarov pistols hung from their belts and each man wore a heavy bulletproof vest.

Major Balbino, the pilot in the lead helicopter, triggered his radio and spoke in Spanish to his counterpart following in the second chopper. "Let me take them out with our machine guns to minimize damage," he said. "Don't fire your rockets unless I give the order. Misses will be bad enough with the machine guns—the rockets will do more harm than good if you miss."

"I understand," the second pilot replied.

As the single-engine Iroquois neared the roof of their target, Balbino toggled the intercom button on his control column to speak to his co-pilot. "Arm our guns."

There was a pause while the co-pilot hit the switches. "Machine guns armed, major."

As the chopper's blades echoed off the sides of the buildings, Balbino knew the rebels would recognize the sound for sure. He initiated a wide S-turn that would loop them around a neighboring building and give them a half circle of the Transamerican Bank. *That should keep the guerrillas guessing which direction we're coming from at least,* the pilot thought.

Halfway through the S-turn, Balbino addressed his co-pilot. "We'll hit them hard, then dive toward the street. The heat waves coming from the pavement should keep us hidden from the Redeyes, if they even have any." He toggled his radio on. "BY-15 this is BY-14. We're going in. Stay clear unless we need you."

"We'll stay clear, BY-14."

The pilot shoved the control forward for maximum speed, completing the half circuit of the Transamerican Bank and lifting the collective pitch lever to bounce them level with the roof. "There they are!" he shouted, his finger slamming the fire button on the control column.

The four machine guns clattered, surrounding the helicopter with a cloud of thin, blue smoke as he crossed the roof, a golden shower of empty cartridges raining down as they passed.

Only a few of the rebels were caught in the fire,

although Balbino had the satisfaction of seeing three crumple to the asphalt roof with his initial pass.

"We're taking ground fire, major," the worried co-pilot warned. "There are rebels hidden behind the concrete guard rail."

"I'll get them," Balbino declared, circling another building to remain hidden and executing a second S-turn that provided them with a different angle of approach toward their target.

"We're starting our second run," Balbino informed the other UH-1H via radio. "I didn't observe any missile launchers, and there're only a few rebels on the roof. We'll wipe them off in no time. Then we'll land and let the *Cinchis* finish them."

"*Excellente,* major," replied the pilot of the second chopper.

Balbino completed his turn and lifted the UH-1H to the level of his target—only to find himself staring at three rocket launcher tubes.

The officer cursed loudly on the intercom, firing a quick burst that spilled one of the rocket operators backward. Then he threw the chopper into a dive as both of the remaining Redeye IIs left their launchers with a bright backblast of fire and smoke.

The leading missile abruptly lost the steeply diving chopper, chasing instead the glare from an office building. It crashed into the glass, penetrated an inner wall, and exploded in a shower of invoices and bills that snowed onto the boulevard below, along with thousands of shards of glass.

"We've shaken the first one," Balbino yelled.

But the second rocket was rapidly gaining on the UH-1H. For a few seconds, the missile lost the descending helicopter in the heat waves that were rising from the asphalt concourse below. But as the aircraft neared the street, Balbino was forced to reduce the speed of the dive. The chopper slowed, passing above a large white semitrailer, which briefly silhouetted the UH-1H from the intense heat emanating from the surface of the pavement.

"I think we've shaken both of them," the major radioed. "The street's protecting us."

At that very moment, however, the Redeye II's homing device locked onto the Peruvian chopper, which contrasted against the cooler surface of the truck below it. The missile rapidly closed on the aircraft's engine exhaust port, striking the rear of the engine. A crippling explosion ripped through the back of the chopper, nearly severing its tail and rupturing its fuel tanks.

The secondary explosion of the fuel demolished the aircraft, which tumbled only meters above the thoroughfare, the fireball of debris sweeping the pavement and engulfing several cars in the rolling inferno.

The crew of the second chopper sighted the huge cloud of smoke rising from behind the Transamerican Bank; the pilot toggled on his radio, fearful he'd receive no reply. "BY-14, come in please. BY-14?"

He waited a few seconds for an answer and then initiated his attack run.

"You sure you're up to the trip?" Father Ramero queried the American geologist.

"Of course I am, now that my ears have quit ringing," Lloyd grinned, the dark bags under his eyes attesting to the contrary. "And Espinoza will help me," he asserted, nodding toward the villager who was smiling broadly, displaying a gap where three front teeth should have been. "Besides," the geologist declared, "we've got to act on this immediately."

"I thought you filed the necessary papers before you came to the village," the priest protested.

"That's true," Lloyd acknowledged, "but this strike is big—super big. This may well be the most massive lode every discovered in South America. The government will want to get its hands on the taxes from it *and* they might be persuaded to send some troops to help protect the village from the Shining Path."

"It would be nice to have someone rout the guerrillas once and for all," Ramero admitted.

"So we can take care of both problems at once?" Espinosa inquired.

The priest frowned. "I'm not so sure how good this turn of events will be for the villagers," he remarked. "I've seen what happens when poor people come into money overnight. It will be spent foolishly."

"We can always return to poverty if we find it more virtuous," Lloyd chuckled. "Even if they squander it, at least they'll have had a chance to buy some of the things they've always wanted. Besides," he added, "I'm planning to invest the money so each villager will receive a monthly stipend—they won't be able to spend it all at once."

Maria flashed a smile at her husband. "And there will be a sewer system and a new school. All the things we have been afraid to even dream about."

"Yeah," Lloyd grinned. "There's enough gold

there to provide us with everything we'll ever want, but I need to get going now. Remember to make sure the villagers get rubble piled over the lode so it's hidden."

"It will be done," Father Ramero promised. "It will remain Piton's secret until you tell the government."

"And keep an eye on Maria," Lloyd added, embracing his wife, even though the pain in his arm caused him to grimace.

"Are you sure you feel well enough to journey?" Maria asked, hugging him tightly and wishing he didn't have to go.

"Yes—although I may not be able to if you break my ribs," Lloyd said, teasing her gently. He gave her a playful slap on the bottom, then addressed the priest. "Espinosa and I are going to head down the trail to Cajamarca before nightfall," he said. "We'll take the train from there, and with any luck, arrive in Lima early tomorrow morning. Everything should be squared away fairly quickly so we'll return within in a couple of days."

The priest smiled grimly. "We certainly scavenged enough armament from the dead rebels to keep their friends at bay for awhile," he remarked, his face clouding over for a moment as he remembered the many broken bodies they'd had to bury in the rocky cemetery below the village. "Godspeed to you both, Lloyd, Espinosa," he said, making the sign of the cross over them. "You'd better be on your way."

Lloyd gave his wife a farewell kiss. "Adios," he said.

13

Rather than engage in fancy maneuvers, the pilot of the second Peruvian UH-1H guided the chopper directly toward the Transamerican Bank, going in low, then swooping upward when he got within rocket range.

He shoved the control column forward, tilting the nose downward to acquire his targets, and discharged a salvo of seven 2.75-inch rockets that hissed from their packs serially.

With horror, the pilot discovered that his aim was slightly off; the first three rockets skirted the roof top and smashed into the structure across the street, ripping into it with triple explosions that sent bricks and glass plunging to the avenue below.

The remaining four missiles hit their intended target, blowing the elevator shaft wide open and ripping gaping holes in the surface of the roof. The pilot circled the structure, keeping the nose of his chopper aimed at the top of the building, but fearful of launching additional rockets unless absolutely necessary, lest he miss again.

Two of the rebels appeared from behind the railing where they'd been hiding, leaned over the low wall surrounding the roof, and fired their Redeyes.

The chopper pilot didn't have time to react.

The missiles crossed the distance between him and the building in a flash of exhaust and crashed into the nose of the UH-1H, ripping the cockpit of the chopper apart; the machine hovered for a moment like a decapitated animal, then tumbled toward the ground.

As the wreckage plunged to earth, the blades of its main rotors splintered against the facade of the building with a grinding snap. Screaming *Cinchis* soldiers leapt from the aircraft, smashing onto the pavement below, then the air was deathly quiet.

On the roof, Zurita turned toward the rebels who had felled the chopper. "Good work, comrades," he exulted. "Stay here and take any more helicopters that come near."

Lopez hefted another Redeye. "We only have a pair of rockets left."

"I doubt they'll be foolish enough to send anymore before nightfall," Zurita answered. "By then we'll have located our hostages and be in a position to bargain for our escape and the freedom of our brothers in the imperialist's prisons."

The two men murmured agreement, their self-assurance bolstered by the destruction of the two Peruvian choppers.

Zurita slammed a new magazine into his rifle, jerked the charging lever to verify that the AKM had a round chambered in it, and headed back downstairs.

*　　*　　*

A passing cloud blotted out the sun, casting a moving shadow onto the buildings below; then the sun broke through as Oz circled the Transamerican Bank from a safe distance, communicating via radio with Commander Warner. "There appear to be no survivors from either of the choppers, Mother Hen. Over."

Warner cursed for several seconds before regaining control of himself. "I've received word from our embassy," he reported, "that the Peruvians want to negotiate with the terrorists rather than try anything else. They definitely don't want you to try to go in."

"Is there any word from on high?" Oz asked, using the code words designating the chain of command leading to the president of the U.S.

"Nothing official," Warner replied. "But the big 'W' is weighing his options. Do you think you could get a rescue party onto the roof? I need to know exactly what you think your chances are. Over."

Oz answered slowly. "It'd be real tough, especially since we don't know the hostages' exact location. We might clear the roof with our machine guns long enough to land," the pilot added, "but it'd be pretty tricky to avoid the Redeyes."

"But there is a chance?" Warner pressed, realizing the State Department would be interrogating him.

"Yes, there is a chance," Oz replied. "But striking the enemy without injuring our people will be very difficult," he cautioned. "So where does that leave us?"

"Given the current administration's don't-give-an-inch thinking about terrorism . . . if you read me," Warner responded. "Over."

"I understand," Oz acknowledged, realizing that Warner had to monitor what he said, even in the comparatively safe transmissions via satellite. President Crane's position regarding terrorism made it a political necessity for the U.S. to attempt to rescue the hostages rather than negotiate with the Shining Path.

"Scout the area again and then get to the embassy so we can talk by secure phone," Warner ordered. "I'll be getting in touch soon. Over and out."

"Captain," Luger called from the gunners cabin, "we've got a flashing light coming from the Transamerican Bank. Top floor, that small window in the center."

"Yeah, I see it, too," Death Song said. "It's morse code!"

"What're they saying?" Oz asked, maneuvering his chopper to a hover and angling slightly to face the distant building.

"I can't believe it," Death Song declared. "B-I-S-H-O-P. It's repeating it again now."

"Agent Bishop?" Oz asked.

"Maybe it's a trick," O.T. suggested. "Maybe the rebels are trying to sucker us in."

"Do you have a signal mirror back there, O.T.?"

"Yeah, I think I've got one in my emergency kit."

Oz smiled to himself. O.T. had one of everything in his emergency kit. "Can you signal them from here if I hover?"

"Yeah, I think so," O.T. replied. "The sun's high enough that we can communicate back and forth. Provided it doesn't cloud up," he added, eyeing the bank of dark clouds half covering the sky.

"Can you communicate without anyone on the roof observing you?" Oz asked.

"That's a good question," O.T. said. "I think so, but I'm not sure how much light's dispersed by one of these signal mirrors."

"We also need to ask a question that only Bishop can answer," Oz told his crew. "We need to know whether we're dealing with the agent or the rebels."

The two gunners headed into the passenger compartment, where Luger slid open the side door. O.T. snapped his headphone plug into the intercom jack and sat on the seat nearest to the open door. He lifted the stainless steel mirror and sighted through the hole in its center, aligning his free hand with the distant window where the word "Bishop" continued to flash.

O.T. shone the sun's reflection from the mirror onto his hand and, satisfied that he was ready, spoke into the intercom. "Any ideas what we should ask, captain?"

The crew was silent as everyone tried to think of some foolproof question. "I've got it!" Oz exclaimed.

O.T. listened to his idea, an amused grin flickering across his face as he started the short and long pattern of morse-code flashes to whoever was in the building.

Bishop found that sending the code was considerably easier than deciphering it from the MH-60K; in fact, he found he was having serious trouble reading the message. "Can anybody else in here read morse code?" he inquired.

Nobody spoke up.

Bishop swore under his breath and turned back

to the window. "S-L-O-W-D-O-W-N" he flashed to the chopper.

The helicopter's signal stopped.

Then the communication came again from the aircraft, this time slowly enough that Bishop was able to keep up, picking out the letters and stringing them together as he decoded them. "Knock, knock?" he asked incredulously, wondering if he'd read the message correctly.

"What the hell's going on?" the vice-president whispered angrily. "What kind of a message is that!"

"Wait a minute," Bishop muttered, an uncharacteristic smile momentarily flickering across his face. "They're making sure we're really Americans and not the Shining Path trying to trick them. They're sending a password challenge."

"I don't get it," Decker said.

He was rewarded with scornful looks from both Bishop and agent Raborn.

Bishop turned to the window and flashed his rejoinder: "Who's there?"

A moment later, he received the reply: "Oz."

Bishop responded: "Oz who?"

Satisfied it was Bishop, the American chopper crew sent: "What's your situation?"

Bishop replied hastily: "Hidden inside washroom. Rebels searching. Will soon be found."

"Should we attempt rescue?"

"Yes. Let us know when."

A dark cloud briefly covered the sun; when it had cleared, a final message flashed from the chopper: "Will return ASAP."

14

Warner directed Oz to the U.S. embassy in Lima, where the two conversed via a safe line connected to a Drid Sac portable "STU-3" telephone. The communications system also possessed a modem feature that allowed a computer to utilize the scrambler; Warner had used the feature to send a packet of diagrams, which were waiting for Oz when he arrived.

"We lucked out on the blueprints I faxed to you," Warner remarked, learning about the message from Bishop. "The secret service insisted on procuring them before they sent the VP to Peru, so they faxed them to us."

"It looks like the delegates and Bishop are hidden in the small lavatory off the conference room," Oz reported to Warner, sliding the blueprints to O.T. to study. "It's hard to believe the rebels haven't found them."

"But I don't think it sounds like a trap," Warner said. "If they had the president of Peru and our vice president, we'd be hearing about it."

"Yeah. I'm pretty sure it was Bishop we were communicating with," Oz agreed.

"All right," Warner said, "here's how it breaks down: First, the Peruvians are ready to bargain as soon as the guerrillas contact them; while their president has been tough on terrorism, the guys presently in charge aren't so inclined. Our State Department's obtained info from the CIA that makes us believe the Peruvians will make major concessions and might even be willing to sacrifice our vice-president, if necessary.

"Second, President Crane is a lame duck, serving his last term in office. He isn't worried about getting reelected. The secretary of state contacted me and told me in no uncertain terms that the president is *not* going to sit still for hostage negotiations with terrorists.

"You and your people are to ignore the Peruvians' instructions, take a Marine contingent from the embassy directly to the Transamerican Bank, and initiate a rescue attempt. This is a direct order from the president of the United States.

"If you succeed in the rescue, our ambassador should be able to smooth the ruffled feathers. But if the president of Peru is seriously injured or killed during the rescue attempt, or you are unable to rescue him for some reason after you make an attempt, then you'll go directly to your transport, which is under orders to take off immediately and head straight for the U.S. If necessary, you will destroy your chopper and leave it at the airstrip.

"Your crews, the air force personnel, and the Marines will be given false papers showing all of you were elsewhere during the time of the rescue attempt, and CIA 'ringers' will be charged with an unauthorized rescue attempt. Your careers, therefore, won't be compromised, plus the ringers will take the heat off the State Department and army. This has already been made clear to the marines, and the ambassador in charge understands, too.

"Now," Warner continued, "the Peruvians aren't going to be too happy to see us go racing in when they've ordered us not to. So one of our CIA operatives there in Lima has departed for an undisclosed location to send a phony radio message on your military frequency; he will pose as a Peruvian military authority and give you the go-ahead via radio to initiate your rescue."

"But the Peruvians will know that the message is a fake, won't they?" Oz asked.

"That is correct, but we're going to conclude that it must have been the Shining Path trying to lure you into a trap. Our argument will be that it isn't your fault that you were fooled by the communication, and that you were trying your best to follow Peruvian orders. It's pretty iffy that this will hold water, but coupled with the ringers it will give us some room in which to maneuver."

"So when I get the message, I'll reply as if I believe it's coming from the Peruvians."

"Exactly," Warner acknowledged. "You'll have to play dumb, even if everything goes smoothly. Stick to the story and we'll support you from our end."

"Okay."

"Any questions?"

Oz thought a moment. "No, sir. We take the marines directly to the roof after getting the fake CIA transmission, then go to the transport and leave if things don't work in freeing the Peruvian president, or play dumb if we rescue him."

"Can you get into the air in ten minutes?"

"Yeah, the chopper's refueled and I can see the marines boarding now," the pilot reported.

"I'll send our CIA radioman the go ahead, then. Once you get his message, switch off your radio immediately so the Peruvians can't reach you."

"Will do, sir."

"Good luck, Oz."

Ten minutes later, the MH-60K was accelerating above Lima, the buildings below darkened by thick clouds which hid the afternoon sun. Oz ignored the case of "shakes" he was experiencing as added adrenaline coursed through his arteries, providing him with a pre-combat surge of energy. He concentrated entirely on his flying.

He navigated the wind currents expertly, flying the chopper low, barely skirting the tallest buildings in the city. The composite graphite epoxy, fiberglass, and titanium blades of the chopper boomed through the air, their echoes reverberating from the structures they passed.

"NS-1, this is Commander Refugio speaking for the *Guardia Republicana.* Come in please," called an official-sounding voice over the radio.

"This is NS-1, go ahead, commander," Oz answered.

"We are giving you permission to assault the Transamerican Bank building to rescue the hostages there," the CIA operative answered. "Our government feels it is imperative that you execute this mission immediately to guarantee the safety of our leaders."

"We read you, commander," Oz radioed back, thinking the operative was really laying it on thick. "We'll head in ASAP, commander. Over and out."

A second radio broadcast cut in on the same frequency, the voice speaking frantically in Spanish and then in English. "NS-1, NS-1, please ignore the orders—"

Oz snapped off the radio and tapped the intercom button. "Gentlemen, arm your weapons; we are heading in."

As the helicopter crew prepared for the attack, the U.S. marines riding in the MH-60K's passenger compartment did likewise. Three of the eight men carried Remington 870 pump shotguns containing "00" buckshot shells; four of the leathernecks packed M16 rifles with low-penetration Federal "Blitz" ammunition. Both ammunition loads were designed to immediately take the fight out of a foe while posing less risk to hostages than conventional ammunition. The eighth marine cradled an M203 grenade launcher with its rifle half loaded with 5.56mm NATO cartridges and an M651 CS tear gas cartridge in its single-shot tube. Extra tear gas and M433 high-explosive cartridges waited in the bandoliers hanging across his chest.

Sergeant Clark Truitt led the contingent of marines. Signaling the seven under his command, they cycled their weapons, placing a live cartridge in the chamber of each firearm and checking that the safeties were engaged.

The marines wore holstered Beretta M9 pistols

and K-Bar knives. Stun, tear gas, and smoke grenades were cached in their flak vests and an M40 gas mask was nestled in its carrier on the left thigh of each trooper.

Truitt signaled again and the men quickly pulled their masks from the carriers with a precision that reflected hours of drill. They jerked the masks across their faces, tugging the rubber straps to snug them. To ensure that the seal was airtight, each man placed a hand on his intake valve and inhaled to collapse his mask. Satisfied, the marines replaced their "Fritz" Kevlar helmets onto their heads.

They were ready to kick ass.

Their battle plan was simple and to the point. The army chopper was to wipe the roof clean so the marines could exit the MH-60K and begin their assault. From there, the chopper was to circle the structure, giving any support possible.

The marines' tactic for taking the top floor of the building was also simple: gas the top floor with the grenade launcher and hand-thrown tear gas canisters, then go in wearing gas masks and kill every terrorist they encountered until the area was secured.

However, executing those simple tactics was going to be difficult, Truitt realized, as he sat in the helicopter and studied his men; they'd do well, he knew, but they'd been trained to defend the U.S. embassy. Going on the offensive was different and considerably more dangerous, especially given the sketchy blueprints of the floor and the little time they'd had to study them. But there was no choice: orders were orders. This had been thrust on them and they'd have to do the best they could.

"Sergeant Truitt," Oz's voice called over the intercom, "we're nearing the Transamerican Bank. They'll probably launch at least one rocket before we can hit the roof with our guns so be sure your men are buckled in. We'll be performing some pretty frenzied acrobatics to lose the missile."

"Yes, sir. Will do," Truitt responded, wondering just how violent the maneuvers of the hi-tech chopper might become. He'd heard the MH-60K was capable of barrel rolls; whether that was correct or not, the fact that people even suggested it probably meant that he and his men were in for quite a ride. "We're secure," he told the pilot.

"Why don't you switch to your radio so we can be sure it works," Oz suggested.

"I'm changing over now, sir," Truitt answered. He removed the headset and put his helmet on. The integral radio built into the headgear positioned an earphone in his left ear; a tiny microphone in the earpiece also transmitted the vibrations coming from his jaw bone, enabling him to communicate via radio even with his gas mask on. "Can you read me, captain?" he asked.

"Loud and clear," Oz answered. "We're almost there. We'll signal our people in the building and then we're going in."

Lopez pointed out the distant MH-60K to Zurita.

Zurita studied the machine for several moments before he spoke. "The chopper is signaling someone in this building with its landing lights."

"Earlier, they were using a mirror," Lopez added.

"You should have told me," Zurita said evenly. "Can you read what they're saying?"

"No," Lopez answered. "But it's a safe bet they're preparing to try something."

"Keep your men alert so you can take the 'copter with rockets if it gets too close," Zurita ordered. "But don't try a long shot; we don't have rockets to waste. I'm going to help with the search. Call me if they try to send another signal."

The rebel leader turned on his heel and headed for the stairs, finding it difficult to believe that they had not yet captured their hostages. He'd expected to lose men, perhaps even die. But to be searching a darkened floor like children playing hide-and-seek! Entering the darkened stairwell and descending to the floor below, Zurita muttered a curse that was old when the Spanish discovered Peru.

He pushed through the double doors and entered the darkened corridor that smelled of death and gunpowder. "Cesar, what have you got?" he asked.

"Nothing, comrade," the rebel replied. "We've searched everywhere, starting from the conference room and working our way through every closet and hallway. They're nowhere."

"And yet someone is signaling from a helicopter," Zurita said, stroking his chin.

"Signaling?"

Zurita nodded. "From outside."

"To view the signal, someone would have to be at a window," Cesar suggested.

"That's true," Zurita agreed. "That means they have to be on an exterior wall and to the east where the helicopter is hovering. Let's search again, starting

with the conference room. I want your men to cover
every inch of wall to be sure there isn't a closet or passageway they missed the first time."

The leader turned and headed for the conference
room, gathering his men along the way.

Bishop waited, listening at the hidden door as the
guerrillas searched the conference room for the second time. It was only a matter of time before they
found the half-hidden door to the lavatory.

Realizing their luck was finally running out, the
agent readied his TEC-9K as the voices of the two rebels grew louder.

Abruptly, the talking outside the hidden entrance
ceased. As one of the rebels scratched at the crack of
the doorway with his finger, he realized there was a
half concealed latch that had been incorporated into
the design of the mural by a skillful artist.

He reached over to the latch and pulled at it. As
the door clicked open, the man raised an eyebrow and
glanced toward his companion.

Before he could speak, a blistering flurry of shots
ripped through the facade of the door, pocking the
rebel with bloody holes.

The second guerrilla raised his rifle, but before
he could trigger the firearm, a second volley punched
him.

The others searching the conference room raised
their weapons.

Inside the hidden restroom, brass from the hot
TEC-9K danced across the floor as Bishop warned the
delegates clustered around him to get to either side
of the door.

The already crowded dignitaries squeezed into the cramped space on either side of the entrance just moments before a barrage of .30-caliber holes cut into the door and smashed into the lavatory. A torrent of water ran out of one of the pipes pierced by a bullet.

A second salvo pounded into the door frame and the nearby wall.

Now we've had it, Bishop thought. Although the wall was fabricated of poured concrete, it was only a matter of time before the powerful rifle bullets chipped through the barrier.

Suddenly a voice cried out above the shooting. When the message had been angrily repeated, the ferocious assault abruptly stopped.

Although Bishop couldn't understand exactly what had been said—it sounded like a native American language—he knew the gist of it: the American vice-president and the president of Peru were to be taken alive.

And the rest of us will be dead meat when that happens, the agent realized, speedily reloading the TEC-9K with his last spare magazine. He crossed to the window and scrutinized the American chopper as it navigated its approach to the building. Turning back, he quickly surveyed the paper towel dispenser next to the hemorrhaging lavatory. "Anybody got a cigarette lighter or a match?" he inquired.

Lopez activated the cooling unit of the Redeye II and sighted at the distant chopper. "I'm sure it's coming in," he told the rebel assisting him. "Have your launcher ready in case the rocket misfires."

Hearing the lock-on buzzer announcing that the

warhead had differentiated the target from its environment, Lopez squeezed the trigger on the launcher's pistol grip. There was a loud hiss as the booster came to life, its back blast blistering the asphalt behind him. As the projectile leaped from its tube, the booster kicked in thirty yards away, sending the projectile flashing toward the American helicopter.

15

As the dark MH-60K sped toward the Transamerican Bank roof, the rolling clouds above looked to Oz like a black sea in a world turned upside down, the lights from the buildings below appearing as stars in the topsy-turvy landscape.

Within seconds, as the Americans were closing with their objective, Oz discerned the telltale launch signature of a missile.

"Rocket!" Death Song warned.

The army pilot pulled instinctively on the collective pitch lever, taking his helicopter upward so fast that, with the additional G-force straining against the frame of the chopper, the crew and passengers were pinned to their seats. The Redeye II followed, homing in on the chopper's warm exhaust manifold.

Having previously armed the countermeasures module, Death Song hit the flare button; the countermeasures pod coughed out a parachute with an infrared flare sputtering to life on the lines. "Flare away," he announced, flipping another switch. "IR jammer activated."

With the flare hanging in the air behind them,

Oz slammed the collective pitch lever down, throwing the MH-60K toward the streets and inducing everyone to hang nearly weightless in their harnesses. He expertly skirted the roof of a building in their path, the blades of the tail rotor whipping so close to the edge of the structure it seemed they would graze the glass and steel.

As the MH-60K plunged past the building, the street came rushing toward them, the noise of the chopper's rotors booming from the facades and echoing down the thoroughfare. Passersby on the street stared upward in horror as the aircraft plummeted toward them.

At the last possible moment, the pilot hauled up on the collective pitch lever, again thrusting the occupants into their seats with the heavy G-forces. The chopper's frame groaned, pushed as it was to its design limits by the stress of the arrested descent.

As the missile that trailed the chopper turned to home in on the flare, the warhead exploded, rocking the city with its thunderclap. A moment later, a light hail of flak rattled harmlessly against the armored skin of the MH-60K.

"I'm taking us back to the bank building," Oz warned. "We'll try to get the jump on them this time." He jockeyed the helicopter through the cavern of buildings they hurtled between. "Be ready with the flares," he told Death Song. "We won't have room for error at the close range we'll be heading in at."

The pilot guided the chopper along the street, rounding a corner as they advanced toward their objective, with the nose of the helicopter facing into the wind. Taking advantage of the increased air speed provided by the breeze, Oz climbed at the maximum rate by throttling the control on the collective pitch, then lifting the lever as he kept the control column forward. The MH-60K leaped skyward, the pilot carefully keeping it on course with the rudder pedals, while skillfully adjusting the collective pitch lever to maintain the full-power lift.

Oz brought the MH-60K into a roll as they topped the building to their left and overflew its roof. The Transamerican Bank building now loomed ahead of the still-climbing chopper. "This is it!" Oz warned the crew.

On the railing above them, Lopez gaped at the machine climbing toward him, his face a study in dismay at the speed of the chopper. "Give me that!" he barked at Sanchez, snatching the Redeye II out of the other rebel's hands. Whirling back toward the chopper, he shouldered the launcher and aimed, switching on the coolant and bracketing the aircraft in his sights. Then his finger stroked the trigger.

At the same instant, Oz activated the dual machine gun pod, discharging the .30-caliber guns and splattering the concrete with bullets as they climbed toward the rebel. In a fraction of a second, the chopper nosed its way upward and aligned its fire on Lopez and the missile.

An explosion ripped across the top of the building, vaporizing Lopez into a cloud of shrapnel, blood, and bone, swept into the air by the blades of the chopper.

As Oz completed the climb and whipped over the roof, Death Song cried out, "We hit the warhead!"

Oz jerked the control column, slamming the collective pitch lever downward to take advantage of ground effect on the surface of the roof. They hovered momentarily above the asphalt, then rotated violently when the pilot kicked the rudder pedal, nosing the chopper to cover two rebels who dashed from the stairwell, their AKMs blazing.

A bullet smashed into the windscreen in front of Oz, lodging in its plastic surface. The pilot jabbed the fire button on the control column, energizing the dual machine guns in their pod and spraying the two rebels with projectiles. The gunmen dropped in their tracks, their rifles clattering against the asphalt.

Luger, spying another guerrilla lifting a LAW-80, centered the rebel in his sights and triggered his Minigun. The man dropped before he could even extend the weapon's launch tube. The gunner released the trigger on his Minigun, glanced around the roof and, seeing no one else, called over the intercom, "All's clear on starboard."

"Port and tail're clear," O.T. announced from the other side of the helicopter.

Oz dropped the MH-60K the last three feet to the roof without fully lowering the collective pitch lever, fearing the damaged structure might not sustain the full weight of the machine. "It's all yours, Sergeant Truitt," he radioed the marine officer.

Truitt signaled his men, who vaulted out of both sides of the chopper and sprinted to the stairwell at the north side of the roof. As Private Colucci, the M203 grenadier, dropped to one knee and discharged his weapon, a 40mm warhead left the launcher and smashed through the distant glass door, flooding the stairs with tear gas.

The chopper behind the marine leapt into the air to circle the building, departing in a burst of speed that buffeted dirt across the surface of the roof. Colucci unlatched the barrel of the M203, shoved the tube forward to eject the empty casing, and pushed a new shell into the chamber.

Rising to his feet, the youthful leatherneck drew the launch tube closed, ensuring that the M203 was prepared if it should be needed. Then he followed the others, who dashed toward the entrance leading to the top floor.

Truitt was the first to dive into the smoke-filled stairwell, his boots scraping the concrete steps; as he bolted forward, he turned his head to and fro for better visibility in the gas mask. Visually sweeping the stairs, he spotted a rebel staggering upward toward him through the smoke, his eyes streaming. The man raised his AKM, intending to fire blindly through the tear gas.

Truitt fired his 870 shotgun first, however, the blast echoing through the stairwell. The buckshot from the shotgun failed to spread little more than an inch, owing to the proximity of the target, but the pellets chewed a jagged hole into the rebel's chest. The man tumbled down the steps, his heart ripped apart.

The marine sergeant racked another cartridge into the chamber of his pump gun and leapt over the fallen rebel onto the landing. He glanced down the remaining stairs and, observing no one, bounded down three steps at a time to the double doors leading to the top floor.

The other marines charged after Truitt, their

boots and equipment creating a deafening riot of noise. As the sergeant neared the entrance, he spotted a guerrilla with a bandanna covering his face pushing through the door to block their advance. The rebel activated his AKM, blazing away in the dim light, sending bullets ricochetting along the walls beside Truitt.

One of the bullets glanced off the officer's helmet, his head torqued by the blow. When the marine recovered, his eyes blinking tears at the pain, he shouldered his shotgun and triggered it.

The pellets slashed into the guerrilla's face, splattering the doors with blood; the man fell backward into the hallway in a shower of broken glass. Truitt hurdled over the fallen rebel, shoving at the frames of the double doors to stumble and cut his hand in the broken glass.

He rolled across the dark passageway beyond, regained his footing, and rose like an acrobat, his shotgun still in hand. Shaking his head in disbelief, he was almost unable to comprehend that he hadn't sprawled on his face.

The other marines clamored into the hallway behind him and the sergeant raised his hand. When the troopers observed the signal, they dropped to their knees, weapons at the ready.

Truitt tapped the transmitter on his helmet, leaving behind a bloody smear from the cuts on his fingers. "We're in," he radioed. "We met only minor resistance and there's no one in the hallway so we're heading on to the conference room."

"Nice going," Oz answered on the radio. "We'll

swing around to get a visual on the conference room from outside."

"Let us know what you see. Over and out," Truitt replied, switching off his transmitter and turning to the grenadier. "Colucci, give me some tear gas at the end of the hall."

The young marine lifted the M203 to his shoulder and fired, the 40mm projectile flashing from the launcher and smashing against the far wall, flooding the area with tear gas.

The explosion was followed by a paroxysm of coughing.

"Sounds like we splashed someone around the corner," Colucci said grimly, chucking another of the large shells into the M203.

"Let's move," Truitt ordered. "Frank, stay here and guard our rear. These walls look thin enough for them to cut a rat hole through."

Truitt rose and yanked a stun grenade out of his flak jacket. "Fire in the hole!" he hollered as he half tossed, half rolled the grenade toward the end of the corridor. As the device bounced to the end of the hallway and exploded, the marines raced in after it.

But they failed to notice the thin cord strung across the hallway ahead of them. Truitt's boot jerked the line, ripping loose the safety rings of the three RGN grenades taped to the molding of the wall, half hidden by one of the bodies.

The corpsman behind Truitt saw the arming handles snapped away from the RGNs. "Grenade!" he screamed, his voice muffled by the gas mask.

The marines surrounding him tried to put as much space between themselves and the device as they could, but several of them were unsure of the weapon's location and collided with each another.

What the devil? Truitt wondered, turning to locate the danger.

The first device exploded, peppering his body with sharp aluminum fragments, one of which cut through his neck between the rear of his helmet and the collar of his flak jacket, severing his spinal column. He was dead before his body fell to the floor.

The other two grenades were tossed into the air by the first explosion and ignited a fraction of a second later at chest level, downing most of the marines. As the smoke cleared, five of the Americans lay by their sergeant, three dead and two unconscious and bleeding profusely.

Only Privates Frank and Colucci remained standing, bleeding from cuts on their arms and faces. They stood in a stupor, gazing down at their injured and dead companions, half hidden by the darkness and smoke.

Although his ears rang, Colucci could hear the clatter of boots around the corner in front him. He gripped his M203 and shouted to his companion, "Here they come!"

Frank produced a flash-bang, withdrew the pin, and tossed it around the corner. Three seconds later, it exploded; both marines leapt out in front of the oncoming rebels, firearms blazing in the near darkness as they assaulted the oncoming enemy.

The five rebels, half stunned by the concussion of the grenade, lost precious moments; trained at snap shooting, the Americans instantly struck the rebels with a heavy barrage, killing three and wounding the other two.

The injured guerrillas reacted quickly, spraying wildly at the two Americans. As six bullets stabbed Private Frank, he toppled over with an agonized groan.

Colucci ignored the hammer-like blow of a bullet to his thigh and pumped the trigger of his firearm for one final three-round burst, cutting down one of the rebels. The leatherneck jerked the trigger once more and realized his rifle was empty.

As the remaining guerrilla fired wildly, Colucci shouldered his M203 and triggered the grenade launcher, sending its huge projectile blooping from its tube and catching the last rebel in the stomach, doubling the man over with its force.

The American grenadier fell to one knee, blood spurting from the ruptured vein in his thigh. His right forefinger released the empty magazine from his rifle, while his free hand clawed a full one from his combat vest; then he slapped the magazine home. He tapped the bolt carrier release button so the bolt snapped forward, chambering a round. Finally, he regained his feet.

Colucci saw another rebel slink from the doorway ahead; but before the marine could raise his M203, Zurita had aimed and squeezed off a burst from his AKM.

The private's rigid muscles threw him backward onto the floor, where he lay, arms and legs twitching spasmodically for a moment before he died, his weapon still gripped tightly in his hand.

Zurita stared at the tangle of American and rebel

bodies littering the hallway then returned to the conference chamber, his face a mask.

"Comrade Zurita, is everything all right?" Cesar inquired.

The rebel leader didn't answer immediately. "We don't have enough time," he finally said, addressing the remaining four rebels in the room. He drew a grenade from his belt. "It's only a matter of minutes before more soldiers reach the roof—and it doesn't appear they're in a negotiating mood. But if we can't take the president, at least we can kill him."

The rebels nodded grimly as they readied their weapons for the final assault on the hiding place of the government dignitaries.

16

Oz skimmed the roof of the Transamerican Bank building to confirm that it was still clear. "Truitt, this is SP-1," he called for the third time. "Do you read me? Over."

When there was still no answer, he switched to his intercom. "We've lost them," the pilot informed his crew.

"Do you think the building is cutting their transmissions?" Death Song asked.

"No. Truitt radioed from the hall," Oz replied. "It looks like they've run into trouble."

"Captain," Luger shouted, "we're getting a signal from the washroom again."

Oz kicked his right rudder pedal to face the conference room.

The exterior glass was still reflective enough to prevent observation of the chamber beyond. The pilot glanced toward the washroom window and noticed flames emanating from deep inside; the blaze was momentarily blocked from view by a toilet stool lid held in front of the window, creating a crude Morse code signal.

Death Song read the message aloud: " 'HIT THE CONFERENCE ROOM REBELS ALL THERE.' "

Oz lifted the chopper into position to hover near the mirror-like glass windows of the meeting hall. *The concussion from a rocket would likely injure the people in the washroom, even with thick concrete walls protecting them,* he deliberated.

That left only the machine guns.

The pilot glanced at the weapons stores display, observing that he still had plenty of ammunition. He activated his machine guns, lightly tapping the left rudder pedal to rotate the nose of the MH-60K as he fired, transversing the glass with a heavy barrage of bullets.

The thick glass shattered, dropping down to the street below and into the conference room, where three rebels remained on their feet after the initial salvo. The men rose and aimed at the chopper.

Oz punched the fire button again, transversing in the opposite direction.

The machine gun pod spit flames, its tracers tearing into the room, pocking furniture and finally cutting down the three rebels, who'd turned to flee.

"See any others?" Oz asked.

"Negative," Death Song answered. "And no one else on the infrared, either. Looks like you got all of them."

"There's another message from the washroom," Luger reported.

Oz watched the small window.

The signal flashed: "YOU GOT THEM WILL MEET YOU ON THE ROOF BISHOP."

*   *   *

When Zurita saw the American helicopter's machine guns open fire on the conference room, there was little doubt in his mind that staying in the chamber meant certain death. He'd leapt through the double oak doors, a bullet whizzing by his scalp as he charged into the hallway.

Nearing the corner, he vaulted over the bodies of Frank and Colucci, rounded the turn, and dashed past the broken bodies of the other U.S. marines lying in a bloody heap.

Pausing at the stairwell, he listened intently.

The noise from the American chopper was growing louder. Realizing it must be landing on the roof, he whirled back toward the elevators that were frozen in place, their power curtailed.

A plan rapidly formed in the rebel leader's mind. Although he knew it was mad, he had little choice; to stay where he was meant certain death. And while he didn't mind dying for the cause, he didn't want to throw his life away for no good reason. Better to live and strike another blow against the hated imperialists than to die needlessly now.

He reached under his poncho.

"Stay here," Bishop warned the delegates. "I need to verify that all the rebels are dead."

"We'll wait," vice-president Decker promised, still sitting on the floor, oblivious to the water drenching him from the spurting water pipe. "Just get us out of here as soon as you can."

"The chopper's heading up to land on the roof now," Bishop told him. "You'll be out in a few minutes." The agent drew his pistol from its shoulder harness and peered cautiously around the door.

No one was to be seen.

He crept out, quietly latching the door behind him and knelt in back of a heavy chair, inspecting the conference room more carefully. Only the dead.

Suddenly, there was a sound in the hallway.

He listened; footsteps crunching through broken plaster.

The agent swore under his breath. *One of the rebels must still be in the building,* he thought. There was no way in hell he was going to allow the chopper to be ambushed—not after telling the army pilot it was clear.

Cursing the rebels' persistence, he raised his pistol and crept across the conference room floor. He quietly shoved his way through the double doorway and dropped to the floor, the doors softly swinging closed behind him, entombing him in the darkness.

Listening intently, he heard the sound of someone dragging something across the floor. Cautiously he crept to the corner of the hallway, raised his pistol in front of him, and carefully peered around the bend in the corridor.

Zurita pushed the stick of dynamite beneath the body of the American agent whom he'd dragged into the nearest elevator; only the fuse leading to the explosive remained exposed.

The Yankee's corpse should deflect the blast downward, he thought morbidly. One stick would be enough to blow the floor out of the elevator car.

If his plan worked at all, it was going to be close.

From the roof above, the loud thumping of the helicopter announced its arrival. *Any minute,* the guerrilla realized, *the floor will be swarming with imperialist soldiers, and then I'll be a dead man.*

With shaking hands, Zurita extracted a book of paper matches and tore one out. Realizing his arm was stiff, he quickly examined it in the dim glow of the emergency light and was surprised to discover he'd sustained a bullet wound sometime during the fighting.

He struck the match and as it sputtered into a glowing flame, he touched the tiny blaze to the fuse.

For a moment it refused to light. Then the wick hissed to life, spitting sparks as it burned toward the explosive charge.

The rebel rose and hurried out of the elevator to stand with his back to the concrete wall beside the shaft, knowing he would be safe there since most of the blast would be deflected by the corpse.

Suddenly there was a sound of one of the rifles that littered the dark passageway clattering into a wall, as if someone had stumbled over it.

Who's that? Zurita wondered, glaring down the passageway.

Was it one of the secret service agents from the conference room? The rebel saw nothing in the darkness but unslung his AKM and held it ready. *Hurry,* he ordered the dynamite.

A shot echoed down the hallway behind him and blew a hole in the plaster next to his head. He dropped to one knee and observed the silhouette of a man standing in the dim light.

Bishop leveled his pistol, aiming more carefully

this time, and fired just as Zurita dropped flat on the floor; the bullet whined along the wall, inches over the crown of the rebel leader's head.

As the guerrilla leveled his rifle at Bishop, the dynamite abruptly exploded.

The hall rocked perceptibly while plaster dust filled the air like a white fog in the dim light. When the faint emergency lights went dead, the corridor was plunged into total darkness.

Zurita threw down his rifle and rose to his hands and knees, crawling blindly and feeling his way to the edge of the now bottomless elevator. He didn't bother to listen for the agent; he knew the Yankee would be moving stealthily toward him in the shadows. Instead, he rose to his feet, standing shakily at the precipice with his toes over its edge.

He took a deep breath, then leaped blindly into the abyss.

His poncho brushed against the few chunks of metal and plastic that had once been the floor of the elevator, and a jagged piece of metal ripped open his cheek as he fell. He continued to drop through the blackness for what seemed to him an endlessly long time, flailing blindly with his arms, trying to locate the steel cable that lay somewhere in the shaft.

The forward momentum of his jump finally carried him crashing into the twin cables, knocking the air from him as he struck the steel lines. He clawed for a handhold in an effort to check his downward plunge, his fingers slipping on the grease that coated the wire cable. Frantically, he wrapped his legs around the cable, ignoring the steel fibers that dug into the skin of his hands and legs.

He continued to plummet through the gloom, gasping in pain from the friction created by the rough steel skidding against his skin; at last he checked his descent, legs, arms, and fingers burned. He hung quietly on the cable, swinging like a human pendulum, the line resonating with a low hum.

He forced himself to loosen his grip and began a swift climb toward the base of the shaft six stories below.

A flashlight beam stabbed the darkness above him, finally impaling him like a fish on a stick.

"You goddam bastard," Bishop shrieked from high above the guerrilla, his voice echoing like thunder.

A deafening flurry of pistol shots filled the void, the bullets ripping into the concrete beside Zurita and stinging his skin with bits of metal. The empty cartridges from the pistol tumbled downward, tinkling on the walls of the shaft like tiny brass bells.

The American's flashlight vanished, plunging the rebel into darkness a moment before his feet hit the bottom of the shaft. He let go of the cable and felt about on the walls like a blind man, searching for an escape from the grimy pit.

Where's the door? he wondered frantically.

The flashlight above him returned, enabling him to see as the beam scattered off the concrete as Bishop attempted to locate him.

"I think he's still down there," a voiced echoed.

Zurita scampered up the short ladder that had been fortuitously revealed to him and reached for the sliding door leading to the basement.

Without warning, a rifle shot rumbled through

the shaft, nearly deafening the rebel with the noise of its discharge. He frantically pushed at the door with bloody hands, which slid on the metal surface; quickly wiping them on his poncho, he tried again.

The door creaked opened a few inches when a second rifle shot filled the shaft and smashed into the door. At the same instant a pain like a hot poker assaulted the rebel's left flank.

Zurita shoved his scraped fingers into the crack and strained with renewed vigor.

The door opened another six inches.

Before the rifleman could fire again, Zurita squeezed through the narrow opening and squinted into a bright flashlight beam on the other side.

"What have we here?" a surprised Peruvian soldier queried in Spanish, staring at the injured rebel leader. Suddenly, it came to the serviceman that he was not looking at one of the delegates who had escaped from the trap laid by the Shining Path, but at one of the fleeing guerrillas. The soldier reached for the pistol holstered at his side.

At the same instant, Zurita lashed the trooper's face with a bloody fist, striking the man in the temple; a swift kick knocked the soldier's legs out from under him. Once the man was down, the guerrilla booted him in the head, creating a pool of blood around the fallen soldier.

The fools, Zurita thought, squatting beside the dead man. *They only left one guard in the basement since the elevator wasn't working.*

He retrieved the soldier's flashlight and pistol that lay beside him on the floor; then the guerrilla leader straightened his stiff body and limped through the twisting labyrinth of heating ducts, wiring, and pipes.

Booted feet clattered down the stairway in back of Zurita as he shoved aside an old box of generator parts to reveal the secret entrance he and his compatriots had used to invade the building.

Was it only hours ago that we entered? he asked himself, dragging the box over the hole above him.

It seemed to him that whole days had passed.

Replacing the box overhead exhausted the last of his strength. He half fell down the steel ladder, crying in pain from the wounds and abrasions on his arms and legs as he dropped. He lay on the dirty concrete for ten minutes, eventually recovering a small portion of his strength.

Then he forced himself to his feet.

He directed the beam of his stolen flashlight across the water, mostly to reassure himself that nothing waited in the shadows, and plunged into the foul stream.

17

Leon Refugio stood behind his desk, unnecessarily adjusting the lapels of his expensive suit as his visitor settled into the leather chair. "And what seems to be the problem, uh, Senor Lloyd?" he asked, groping for his visitor's name.

"You tell me!" the American answered in Spanish, shifting his huge frame to the edge of his chair. "I've spent the last two days talking to your lackeys, trying to get someone to realize what it is we've discovered. Look at this!" He stood up and emptied his sample bag onto the papers spread over Refugio's desk.

The assistant chief of the ministry of mining and minerals reddened with anger as the dirty chunks of rock spilled onto his desk. Then it came to him what the samples were and his anger evaporated immediately. Cursing softly under his breath, he picked up the biggest of the specimens and inspected it.

"These are not individual nuggets," Refugio remarked, noting the sharp edges where a tool had cut through the yellow metal.

The American said nothing.

"They are from a single lode, no?" the assistant minister asked.

Lloyd nodded.

"And the lode must be nearly pure, judging from the color and weight."

The geologist smiled for the first time in days, recognizing that the official actually knew something about mineralogy.

"We've discovered a giant mother lode, easily the biggest ever found in the western hemisphere," Lloyd explained. "And there are three major veins branching from it; all appear to stretch far into the rock around the deposit."

"Purity?"

"Nearly all of it is as pure as the samples you're looking at."

"And you need a company to handle the operation?"

"I've already contacted the Dorado Mining Company and they've agreed to handle the operation."

"You've made a good choice," Refugio remarked, replacing the sample and perusing the papers Lloyd had brought in with him. "It says here you've already secured mining rights from the government—years ago, in fact." He tossed the papers onto his desk. "Senor Lloyd, I don't understand what it is you want from the ministry of mining and minerals."

"The location of the deposit is thick with the *Sendero Luminoso*. They've attacked our village twice during the last week alone. Now that we're starting a mining operation, they'll be like vultures."

"And you want . . ."

"And I want the government to give us protection," Lloyd finished. "We'll be adding plenty of cash to the Peruvian coffers *if* we can engage in mining operations. But if we can't, we lose our livelihood and the government loses a ton of taxes."

"Senor Lloyd, a week ago, you would have been out of luck," Refugio said, a smile blossoming under his drooping moustache. "But with the recent attack on our president and the American delegation, our two countries have come to a joint resolution to fight the Shining Path terrorists with American aid."

"Then someone in the government might help us?"

The assistant chief nodded. "Right now our government and the Yankees are looking for a way to make a gesture—a *declaracion*—that signifies that the rebels cannot control us or hold our country hostage."

"This would do exactly that!" Lloyd said excitedly. "The village is poor; I've created a trust to give the money from the operation directly to the Indians. So it would be a good project for the government to support, since it will put Peru on the side of the Indians rather than the big land owners."

Refugio gripped the armrests of his chair as the American continued to talk. *This will be a good way to secure favor with the minister,* the bureaucrat told himself exultantly. If only he could get word of the operation's needs to the appropriate parties before the government committed itself to another project.

"Uno momento," Refugio interrupted the American. "Senor Lloyd, you needn't say more. I am convinced. Now let me make a phone call and see if we can secure the protection for your operation."

"That would be great!" Lloyd said.

"If you'll excuse me." The assistant chief rose and strode off to another office, forcing himself not to run. He reached the phone, paused to collect himself, and dialed a number at the government palace, where the president and his staff resided.

"Dr. Lloyd!" American Ambassador Paul Dorian declared, grasping the geologist's rough hand in a strong grasp. "I've been hearing a lot about you the last few hours. Sounds like you've stumbled onto quite a find, sir. Have a seat," he said, indicating one opposite his own.

Lloyd bristled at the suggestion that he'd stumbled onto the find after methodically searching for it for years. "Actually, I've been looking for the gold for a long time," Lloyd said.

"Of course, of course you have," Dorian soothed. "Now, Dr. Lloyd, we've been working with the Peruvians," he plowed on, settling into one of the carved chairs in the small embassy suite. "And while the U.S. can't supply troops—too much fear in Congress of another Vietnam or Kuwait commitment— we *can* support you monetarily. We can also give you coverage through a private company that's been trying to market a hi-tech weapons system to the Peruvians."

"Not mercenaries?" Lloyd asked.

"No, not at all," the ambassador reassured him. "We've got sales representatives from Osbourn-Newport—the U.S. airplane manufacturer—who've recently branched into small arms. The company's been demonstrating a new system to the government trying to secure new sales."

"I don't think we can afford to purchase any weapons," Lloyd said.

"No, no. Nothing like that," Dorian again assured him. "They wanted to field test their weapons in actual combat. With the possibility of an attack by the Shining Path, this is the perfect chance for the company. And they'll do it at no cost."

Lloyd said nothing, unsure how good a deal it really would be to have hot-to-trot weapons manufacturer's representatives in his village.

"At least consider it," the ambassador encouraged. "The two sales reps know their stuff—both have army backgrounds—and the weapons are automated and radar controlled. They'd give you a lot of added firepower."

"I'll certainly consider it," Lloyd promised.

"The U.S. government is also going to give you some help," Dorian added. "Since the Peruvian military is taxed to the limit with the new Shining Path offensive at Cusco," he reported, "they can't spare any choppers to get you back to your village. So the vice-president has suggested we have the helicopter team that delivered him to his ill-fated meeting transport you and a contingent of *Cinchis* to your village to help secure it until the *Guardia Republicana* troops can reach your town overland."

"That's very generous," Lloyd said, surveying the blond American army officer who had entered the room, closing the mahogany door behind him.

"Ah, here's your 'copter pilot now," Dorian said, rising to his feet. "Dr. Lloyd, this is Captain Jeff Carson—better known as Oz. Oz, Dr. Harlan Lloyd."

"Dr. Lloyd," the chopper pilot said, shaking hands with the red-haired giant.

"Please call me Lloyd—like my villagers do," the geologist smiled. " 'Doctor' is too stuffy."

"Oz will be transporting you to your village," Dorian continued. "In fact, I think they're on standby now. And if memory serves me correctly, Dr. Lloyd, you have a lovely wife waiting for you back home. I'll bet you'd like to abandon us bureaucrats and return to your friends."

"Yes, sir," the geologist admitted. "I am quite anxious to depart. How soon could you have us in the air?" he asked the pilot.

"Within an hour," Oz answered. "*If* the field reps can get their hi-tech gadgets ready for transport as quickly as they've promised," he added.

"Do you want to take their equipment along?" Dorian asked, rising to his feet.

Lloyd nodded affirmatively. "We might very well need all the firepower we can muster," he confided. "I ought to at least see what they've got."

"I'll have the chopper team plan on staying in your village a couple of nights, in case you want to send the salesmen home," Dorian said.

"Are you sure you can spare the helicopter?" Lloyd asked.

"Oh, sure," Dorian beamed. "The vice-president will be tied up at least that long finalizing the wording of the joint resolution. Besides, the chopper has a for-midable amount of firepower if you should need it," he added. "By the time they have to leave, the Peru-vian military should have reached your village over-land."

"Great," Lloyd said, rising to his feet as they all shook hands and prepared to depart. "Espinoza and I will be ready to go in an hour, Captain Carson," the geologist promised. "Ambassador Dorian, thanks so much for your help in cutting through the red tape and getting things arranged for us. It's people like you who make me miss the states."

"The pleasure has been mine," Dorian replied graciously, putting his hand around the geologist's shoulder and escorting him to the door. "I hope everything works out for you and your adopted people."

"Thank you, sir," Lloyd said, again shaking the ambassador's hand and hastily departing for his hotel.

CHAPTER

18

As Oz levelled out the MH-60K over Lima, O.T. spoke to the pilot over the intercom. "Hold her steady, captain," the gunner cautioned, unbuckling his seat belt. "Luger and I are going aft to shut the side doors; otherwise, I think our dogs may be frozen by the time we get there."

"Commander Warner said good gunners are hard to come by these days," Oz replied, poker-faced, "so I'll try not to dump you two out."

"Appreciate the sentiment," O.T. deadpanned, pulling his helmet plug from its jack.

Although it had been warm on the ground when they'd taken off, the morning air above the city was nippy, thanks to a cool breeze drifting in from the distant Andes. The sky was completely empty of clouds—a perfect day for flying, the pilot reflected.

Three members of the *Cinchis* team riding in the chopper's passenger compartment reminded Oz of several of the soldiers he'd ferried in Vietnam, some of whom had worn the same hundred-yard stare of troops who'd seen excessive combat. The members of the highly trained force carried a minimum of equipment to prevent their movements from being hindered in combat.

The majority of the *Cinchis* were armed with AKRs; two carried BG-15 40mm grenade launchers mounted on the handguards of their carbines, while another sported a heavy RPK-74 squad automatic weapon. All wore lightweight camouflage uniforms.

Sergeant Roque Luis led the eight-man team, and for no apparent reason, Oz had taken an instant dislike to the wiry, reticent Peruvian soldier. *When you get right down to it,* the pilot admitted to himself, *I don't much care for the looks of this team.* They seemed capable enough to the pilot, but the American vaguely suspected them of being untrustworthy or even ruthless; he resolved to avoid the special troops as much as possible once they reached their destination.

Oz found his other four passengers somewhat more agreeable.

The geologist appeared to be, as O.T. had put it, "a gentle giant of a man"; his crooked grin had immediately disarmed the American crew, and they admired his goal of modernizing the village. The native American accompanying Lloyd obviously revered the geologist and quickly endeared himself to the Yankees with his somewhat toothless grin and his habit of gaping out the side window at the ground rushing past below.

The two Osbourn-Newport sales representatives looked like Mutt and Jeff.

Richard Addison was the short, dumpy half of the team who seemed to do all the talking. He referred to "fields of fire" and the "kill/wound" ratios of the hi-tech weapons he peddled as if he were talking about the weather, seemingly impervious to the carnage that his automated weapons were capable of inflicting. From that standpoint, the gregarious salesman was nearly as chilling as the *Cinchis,* and Oz suspected the man's matter-of-fact attitude toward killing had turned off more than one potential customer.

But there's really no telling, the pilot mused, since most of the government paper pushers who adopted and purchased combat equipment were far removed from the flesh-and-blood reality of modern warfare. So Addison's enthusiasm for mechanized slaughter might make him a crack salesman among the bureaucrats.

The other representative, Bill Conrad, was as tall and skinny as Addison was squat and dumpy. All Conrad had in common with his business associate was an identical shaggy moustache that hung over his upper lip and a passion for the weapons system he was peddling.

Conrad was the mechanical whiz in charge of maintaining and programming the sales samples, available for demonstration to any government interested in the futuristic weapons. He traveled in stained coveralls that hung on him like they'd been borrowed from a scarecrow's wardrobe.

Their hardware was slung in a large crate beneath the MH-60K, where it hung suspended with several smaller cases of ammunition on the chopper's heavy cargo hook.

According to the enthusiastic descriptions Addison offered, the XG-223 weapons system was a scaled-down version of the Phalanx CIWS system used on naval vessels to defeat incoming missiles. The

Osbourn-Newport guns were chambered for the NATO-standard 5.56mm cartridge, each unit possessing four motor-driven 20-inch barrels coupled together like a Gatling gun.

A radar/computer link-up combined with a servo-motor enabled the weapon to scan an area with a radius of 1,000 meters and, upon detecting anything man-sized or larger moving within 800 meters, would lock onto the target and saturate it with a deadly volley. Addison also claimed the units could stop incoming mortar shells.

The four XG-223s slung under the MH-60K were to be deployed around Piton once the Peruvian/American contingent landed in the village. According to Addison, the machines would serve as "robotic sentries" to pick off guerrillas unfortunate enough to enter their kill zone.

Oz hoped the machines didn't run amuck.

He'd seen more than one "hi-tech" gadget fail miserably in combat—often with the loss of human life. O.T. had secretly proposed a wager among the helicopter crew—ten-to-one odds—that the first casualty of the Osbourn-Newport weapons would be a villager's llama or goat—and he'd had no takers on his bet.

"We're back in our harnesses, captain," O.T. announced over the intercom, breaking Oz's reverie. "Both side doors are buttoned shut."

The pilot checked his VSD. "We should be refueling in about an hour-and-a-half. Let's keep everyone on board so we can get in and out in a hurry. In the meantime, keep a sharp lookout—there're still a lot of Redeye IIs floating around somewhere down there.''

"Roger," O.T. answered, glancing at Luger, who was already staring out of the open gunners window. His helmet visor was lowered to protect his eyes from the sun as well as the air that whipped past.

Because the operating radius for the MH-60K was three hundred kilometers maximum without external tanks, the American helicopter was scheduled to land at the Peruvian military supply depot north of Cajamarca. Once refueled, it would be a short hop of just twenty-four kilometers to Piton—although it was a much longer trip over land due to the poor, winding mountain roads leading to the village.

By choosing to refuel rather than using an external tank system, the MH-60K crew was able to fly the mission fully armed. The armament mounted to the modified external tank suite struts consisted of what had become more or less the standard armament for the Night Stalkers missions. On the starboard rack perched a pod containing double 7.62mm machine guns next to a twelve-tube 70mm rocket launcher.

To the port, four Rockwell International Hellfire missiles hung on their carrier. The rockets would be guided to their targets with a laser target acquisition and designation sight coupled to an aiming system mounted on Death Song's helmet. A 532 countermeasure flare and chaff dispenser completed the ensemble on the left pylon.

Oz lifted the chopper over a low foothill and dropped gracefully across a jagged formation of sandstone boulders, weaving through the dry basin to present only a minimal target. The olive green MH-60K darted across the plateau like a giant dragonfly, its shadow chasing across the rough ground below; abruptly the shadow seemed to climb a cliff face as if trying to ascend into the sky after the chopper.

The pilot glanced at his watch and wondered what was in store for them during the next few days.

The stolen penicillin Zurita ingested had destroyed the microscopic fauna in his intestinal tract as well as the bacteria infecting his wounds, so the antibiotic upset his stomach and gave him a bad case of diarrhea. Feeling miserable, he limped into a darkened room decorated like a bordello.

"Please sit," the figure in the velvet chair at the rear of the room said in ancient Incan, indicating an overstuffed, crimson armchair situated next to a plaster lamp shaped like a dancing girl.

Zurita hobbled to the chair, stifling a groan as he sat down.

Comrade Berto remained seated, his bald head glistening in the dim light. He adjusted his thick glasses, straightened up in the chair, and placed a cut crystal wine glass on the low table next to him.

"I understand you're in great pain, Comrade Zurita, both from your wounds and the spiritual distress of losing your men," the leader said in Spanish. "Your affection for your men—and your sensitivity— are well known and admired by many in our organization."

"I'm sorry I failed, Comrade Berto."

The room was deathly quiet except for the ticking of a clock. Berto's eyes were riveted on Zurita. "There is failure and there is failure," he said, smiling abruptly and running his finger around the rim of his glass. "Now, both the Yankee and Peruvian governments comprehend just how dangerous we can be. Already there have been calls from the leftists in the U.S. Congress for withdrawal from our country; one even referred to our struggle as a civil war. So we have made progress—thanks to your efforts."

"But I should have done better," Zurita lamented, grimacing as he shifted uncomfortably in his seat.

Berto smiled again. "Would you be interested in striking another blow against the capitalists—while extracting personal revenge at the same time?"

"Certainly."

"Unfortunately we don't have time to wait for your wounds to heal; Comrade Gonzolo feels you are the sole individual capable of performing this job. You will have to push yourself—the mission demands immediate action."

"I have seen men work for our cause in much worse physical condition than I'm in, comrade. Compared to a man tortured by the *Guardia Republicana*, I'm in great shape."

Berto threw back his head and produced a barking laugh, which just as abruptly ceased. "Yes. And if we didn't think you could handle this task, we wouldn't ask you. No one else knows the Cajamarca region well enough to succeed in this mission."

"And what is the mission?" Zurita asked.

"Our operative in the ministry of mining and minerals has reported that a huge deposit of gold has been discovered in Piton," Berto confided to the revolutionary.

"The tiny hamlet that refuses to pay taxes to my men?"

"Exactly. The Peruvian dictators have decided to utilize the village as an example of how they can keep us out."

"And line their pockets with the gold," Zurita added bitterly.

"Plus, the Americans will be helping to protect the village."

At this news, the rebel operative snickered knowingly.

"You'll also be interested to learn, comrade, that the Yankee chopper team that defeated your men at the Transamerican Bank will be carrying a team of *Cinchis* into the village, in addition to the American geologist who made the find. A large convoy from Lima will eventually relieve the *Cinchis,* but it won't arrive for about a week."

"If *that* quickly!" Zurita exclaimed. "Those are some of the worst roads in Peru. You want me, then, to deal with the smaller contingent of Americans and *Cinchis* before the larger pack of vultures gets there?"

"That is correct."

"Kill as many of them as we can?"

"Kill villagers and Americans as you see fit—an example needs to be made of them. But after you take the village, I want you to grab as much of the gold as you can. We have a group of our men coming in from the north, but they won't reach Piton until the day after you arrive."

"They know the location of our camp?"

"Yes, they will meet you there."

"But I don't fully understand," Zurita said.

"How can we operate a mine? I have no experience in that area. Plus, wouldn't it take too much time?"

"There apparently is one huge, nearly pure lode that's exposed at the surface," Berto answered. "If this is true, you should be able to dynamite some large chunks clear to carry back on the villagers' pack animals. Then you must dynamite the vein to conceal it for a while."

"Even if we blow it sky high," Zurita contradicted, "it shouldn't be too difficult for the authorities to find."

Berto smiled. "That's where the American geologist has played into our hands. He has kept its exact location a secret. He's afraid someone else will exploit it before he can."

"But if no one knows its location?"

"You will have to uncover that before you kill the geologist or too many of the villagers."

"There *are* ways to make people share their secrets," Zurita remarked darkly, "and we'll only need one canary."

"That's true," Berto agreed. "Surely you'll have no trouble convincing a villager to share with us." The rebel leader smiled brightly and lifted his wine glass to his lips. "Unfortunately, we've lost contact with the revolutionary cell you left behind in Cajamarca, but we have reason to believe they're about to attack Piton again."

"That's right!" Zurita exclaimed, jerking reflexively and grimacing at the pain. "If only there were some way to stop them until I can get there to consolidate our attack! You do have men who can accompany me?"

"It doesn't matter if they go ahead and attack without you," Berto insisted. "I have reserved one hundred men to serve you, and the second force from the north has an additional fifty men. Both contingents are combat veterans and generously armed," he continued. "Your group will also have the remaining Redeyes and LAW-80s you captured to deal with the American chopper and village brigade."

"The people in Cajamarca that we've lost contact with—will an attack by them pose a problem to our mission?" Zurita asked.

"I don't see how," Berto answered. "If nothing else, they should kill a few more of the villagers before you get there. And if you leave at once, you might be able to prevent a fruitless attack. Comrade Zurita, can you do this for me?"

Zurita rose on shaky feet. "Consider it done, Comrade Berto. We'll deal with Piton and bring back enough gold to help promote the Fourth Sword of our revolution for some time to come."

"One more thing," Berto said, getting to his feet.

Zurita watched as he crossed to a dark corner behind a cabinet and retrieved a long-barreled rifle with a scope mounted on its receiver.

"Comrade Gonzolo wanted me to see that you received the Dragunov you requested."

"You found one!" Zurita gasped, unable to hide his joy. Taking the rifle in his hands, he caressed it as he inhaled the agreeable aroma of gun oil, ignoring the pain in his shoulder. He lifted the SVD sniper rifle, placed his cheek against its skeletized, anatomical stock, and sighted at one of the garish lamps. The rifle felt like it had been custom designed for him. Lowering the firearm, a tired smile lit up his lined face.

"We've also secured a case of cartridges for the gun," Berto said, producing the box from the cabinet. "In fact, finding the ammunition was harder than getting the rifle. From what I hear about your shooting abilities, Comrade Zurita, I think you'll be able to put this rifle to good use."

"Yes, sir, I think I can."

"Then go and further the revolution!"

"You've heard the radio report," Glorimar told the guerrillas surrounding him on the boulders encircling the campfire. "Zurita's plan failed and only one of his men escaped." The rebels nodded glumly.

"Perhaps Zurita was the one who escaped," Pedro suggested.

"He never runs away!" another argued.

"He undoubtedly was among the dead," Glorimar agreed. "So we must attack the village to make them pay their taxes so the other towns don't try to keep their money from us. We must do just as he directed before he left."

"I say we should wait until we hear from his superiors," Pedro said, shifting the scuffed AKM he held in his arms. "What if they no longer want us to attack the village? What if their plans have changed?"

"Why wouldn't they want us to attack?" Glorimar demanded. "You think our superiors like it that a bunch of peasants led by a gringo can hold us in check? That Yankee has made fools of us for too long. We'll be a laughing stock if we don't attack and at least even the score."

"They have made us look bad," Pedro agreed, pulling nervously at his worn poncho.

"It's settled then; we attack!" Glorimar declared, checking his watch. "In thirty minutes, comrades."

"So soon?" Pedro protested.

Glorimar cursed in frustration. "You want to stumble through the dark and see if you can fall prey to their booby traps again?" he demanded.

"Our one chance for success is to go in during the day when we can see where we're walking," another of the rebels reminded Pedro.

Glorimar glared at Pedro, daring him to disagree.

The scarecrow of a man didn't speak or look up; he knew when he was beaten.

"In thirty minutes, then," Glorimar said. "Pedro, you come and help me with our remaining mortar. This time, we *will* take the village," he vowed, "so that those who died in the previous attempts won't have died for nothing."

19

"Heavenly Father," Ramero prayed half aloud as he knelt at the crude stone altar inside the empty chapel. "It's fortunate you've given us gold, because everyone's too frightened to go to the fields or care for their goats. My flock is staying within the stone fence as if we're a city under seige. Please keep the Shining Path evil away from us. You realize I'm tired of burying your children," he added with a shudder, deciding not to mention the body parts of the rebels they'd discovered and been unable to piece together.

He forced the memory from his mind to continue his prayer.

"And help us to survive and let our problems bring us closer to Your plan for us. In the name of the Father—Oh, and please return Senor Lloyd to us soon. He should have been back yesterday and he's the only one that seems to be able to lead the people of our village in their resistance.

"Heavenly Father, you've seen how I try to organize them. But it seems to me that you didn't bless me with the skills needed to lead men into battle. So please return the American to us soon."

The cleric crossed himself, ending his prayer in Latin as he often did when under stress.

He turned from the altar and, as he stood, fumbled with the Exactor pistol twisted inside his robes. *Ah, if my pacifist bishop could see me now!* he thought. *The church refused to remember the past popes who led the holy saints into battle,* the priest reflected. *If today's clergy had been running things in the Middle Ages, Europe would be speaking Arabic and muttering prayers to Allah,* he told himself. This was no different. Only this time the struggle to preserve the faith was against the Godless communists.

He continued to fuss with the lightweight, mostly plastic Ram-Line .22 pistol Lloyd had given him. But since it lacked a holster, the firearm remained hidden beneath his robe, hanging from a string tied about his waist. It was always becoming tangled in his garments—very inconvenient, to say the least. But with the recent troubles with the rebels, he dared not leave it elsewhere.

Finally he succeeded in untangling the pistol, thankful that no one was in the sanctuary to witness the battle with his clothing. He paused to extract his pocket watch from the pouch on his sash, then crossed to the front entrance of the church.

"Ten A.M.," the priest remarked after consulting his timepiece, his voice echoing from the rock face of the tiny sanctuary; time to see that the guards on the *punta* were relieved by the second team. Today the cleric was the solitary villager capable of telling time since he was the only one in Piton with a pocket watch.

And that's not without its burdens on cloudy days like this when reckoning the time by the sun's position is impossi-

ble, he thought to himself. Then everyone expected the cleric to inform them of the correct hour.

If Harlan Lloyd had his way, everyone would have a watch—maybe even electric clocks hanging on the walls. *Real civilization!* Ramero thought, grimacing at the idea. He feared that the villagers would become jaded, wanting more and more of life's luxuries.

Materialism was a curse he'd once experienced himself, he realized. The hardest part of becoming a priest had been divesting himself of his meager possessions. And he'd seen native American families ripped apart when they came into a little wealth.

Unfortunately, it was impossible to increase the villagers' standard of living by small increments and then stop. Once started, they would want more like everyone else. If only—

"Father!" a female voice shouted from the door.

The priest turned to observe Maria dashing toward him, her *mantas* flapping in the wind. "Father, the sentries have spotted a group of the guerrillas coming from the south, climbing toward our village."

"Perhaps they're mistaken and it's Lloyd—" he began.

"No," she shook her head. "The men have guns and they're attempting to conceal themselves. It's another band of rebels."

"Go ring the bell to alert everyone," Ramero directed. Then he rushed out of the church toward the stone wall closest to the approaching rebels.

Moments later the priest arrived at the southern perimeter where the villagers were already collecting, worriedly fingering their rifles and shotguns as the priest paused to inspect them.

Those holding their newly acquired AKMs looked confident—too confident, the priest warned himself. The men seemed to believe the weapons captured after the failed attack made them invincible.

"Remember that the previous owners of your AKMs got their heads blown off," Ramero reminded them. "And the same thing can happen to you. You'll still have to stay down and conserve your ammunition if you are to survive. I'm very tired of burying people in our cemetery, so you work at staying alive."

The priest took one of the rifles from its owner. "And set your selectors to semiauto," he said, sliding the lever on the receiver of the gun away from full-auto setting. "You'll hit them if you aim instead of spraying the countryside with bullets." Ramero felt a sense of déjà vu, recalling how a drill sergeant had done the same for him during his misspent youth. He handed the rifle back to its owner.

A pealing erupted from the church steeple, more tinny than usual since the crack continued to split toward the crown of the bell with each blow off the clapper. The cleric ignored the gradual destruction of his church bell and turned to stare down the slope below the village.

Not having time to create booby traps is going to make the fight tougher for us, Ramero confessed to himself. The village forces would be in static lines along the walls, at the mercy of the rebels. *Lloyd should be here to help us,* the priest realized hopelessly.

"There they are," Jose announced, standing at Ramero's right. The villager pumped a cartridge into the chamber of his Mossberg with a loud clack. Others raised their rifles to the top of the wall and aimed, safeties clicking off along the line.

"Remember to hold your fire until they're very near to us," the cleric cautioned. He gazed at the trail leading toward them and could see the rebels now, stealing from boulder to boulder in an effort to avoid detection. The priest spoke emphatically to the villagers. "Don't shoot until they reach the bend in the path."

"Father," Jose whispered. "There, by the bush. More are coming from that direction."

"Yes, I see," Ramero acknowledged. *How I wish we'd gotten that area booby trapped!* he yearned.

He started at the sound of gunfire. From atop the *punta*, Ernesto shot a short burst with his Czech ZB30 LMG at the distant rebels; the bullets raised a cloud of dust around the guerrillas and one sprawled across a boulder, seriously wounded if not dead.

The villagers cheered and started firing.

"Hold your fire!" Ramero yelled, racing alongside the stone wall, his robe flapping. "They're too far away for our rifles. Save your ammunition—or you'll be out when you need it. Stop firing!" he commanded.

Finally the fusillade stopped.

This isn't going to work, he fretted, returning to his original position at the wall. The villagers were going to exhaust their ammunition before the revolutionaries got into range.

"Father," Saluo the messenger boy whispered to the priest, tugging at his robe.

"What?"

"The *Sendero Luminoso* are climbing the west slope!" the boy exclaimed.

"Are the villagers on that side ready for them?" the priest asked.

"Nearly everyone has come to this wall," the boy said, his eyes wide with fear. "Just a few—"

Ramero muttered under his breath, pivoting on his heel and treading the line again, tapping villagers on the shoulders. "You and you, go to the west wall," he directed. "Some of the rebels are coming from that direction. Get back to the other wall again quickly."

He continued his march along the perimeter, weeding out the villagers who'd crowded in, hoping to repel the invaders from their village.

The priest finally returned to the place where Saluo waited. "Climb up to Ernesto and be sure he's aware of the approach of the rebels from the west."

"Yes, father," Saluo obeyed.

The cleric watched the boy scamper toward the *punta* towering behind the village. When the youngster was halfway up the rocky path, the whistling of a falling mortar round caught Ramero's attention.

Heavenly Father, have mercy, the priest begged, aware of the child's peril. The round exploded near the boy, and Saluo vanished in the cloud of dust.

"Dear God!" the cleric cried, hitching up his robes to get to the youngster. He stubbed a toe against one of the rocks on the hillside but ignored the pain, fastening his eyes upon the prone figure he could barely make out in the dust. Covered with dirt and cuts, the boy looked dead to Ramero. He bent over the child and scooped him up, cradling him gently in his arms. Tears of remorse fell on the boy's dusty face.

The child stirred slightly.

"Oh, Heavenly Father!" Ramero cried, unable

to adequately express his joy that the boy was still alive.

As a distant cough announced the launching of another mortar shell, the priest clasped the boy tightly to his breast. Frozen in place, he debated the probability of whether the mortar crew had launched the same trajectory or a new one. If the shell came over the same ballistic arch, it would land nearly on top of them; if it had been changed, it would be safest to stay put since moving could endanger them.

The priest closed his eyes and, without thinking, began to recite the "Hail Mary," the words tumbling from his lips of their own volition, accompanied by the distinctive whine of a descending shell.

The explosion shook the village.

Ramero opened his eyes to see one of the distant one-room huts in the village torn apart. A moment later, broken bits of tile and rock pelted the priest, somehow reminding him of the stoning of Saint Stephen.

The cleric sighed, realizing the rebels had indeed readjusted their mortar. He clutched the boy tightly and scanned the village as another mortar began its whistling fall.

The round exploded farther back in the hamlet. From the crest of the *punta,* the thumping of Ernesto's LMG rumbled its angry answer to the blast, firing down the western slope leading to the village.

With a sick feeling in the pit of his stomach, the priest realized what the rebels' target was: the machine-gun nest atop the horn of rock. And if they hit it, Ramero knew, the villagers would lose a great advantage. They would no longer have the powerful weapon to fire downward from the *punta* toward the approaches to Piton.

Stricken with horror, Ramero stood holding Saluo in his arms, gazing at the *punta*. The mortar shell dropped in a blur, plummeting directly onto the machine gun nest, blowing Ernesto and his crew from its surface in a cloud of flames and smoke.

Around the hamlet, the sound of the villagers' firing ceased as they looked toward the horn of rock, realizing what had happened. Sadly, they turned back toward the guerrillas and resumed firing with renewed intensity.

Ramero studied the nearest wall. He could see the rebels were still far away, beyond the range of the villagers' rifles. *The guerrillas are drawing our fire, waiting until we've exhausted of our ammunition,* the priest realized helplessly.

There was little doubt in the cleric's mind that within the hour, the rebels were going to launch their final assault and overrun the village.

After entrusting Saluo to one of the women, the priest raced around the perimeter wall like a madman, achieving little. Within ten minutes, the rebels were amassing for their decisive strike.

"No!" Ramero warned the last of the villagers still standing at the wall. "Don't shoot anymore. Not until they're right on top of us."

Jose turned and looked at the priest as if he were mad. The rebels were storming the wall! Surely this was the time to be shooting. "They're less than a hundred meters from us this very moment!" he protested.

"Hold your fire," the priest repeated, peering

over the wall at the attackers who were advancing under the safety of a heavy barrage of bullets. *They're converging on the hole they blew into the perimeter with their last mortar shots,* the priest reflected angrily.

"Come on," Ramero shouted at Jose. "Maybe we can still block them." The two men raced along the wall toward the hole, aware that most of the villagers were retreating into the village to hide, their weapons exhausted of ammunition.

As they reached the breach in the wall and knelt beside it, the priest drew the Exactor pistol from his robe. He pulled its charging ears to the rear and released the bolt, chambering it with a minuscule .22 LR cartridge.

Now I know how David felt, he thought grimly, *except these Goliaths are equipped with AKMs.* Peeping from behind a large boulder, he finally gave Jose the word. "They're close enough now!" he hissed.

The two men rose.

Oblivious to the bullets cracking past him, the priest aimed and fired. One of the rebels staggered and dropped his rifle, clutching at the tiny red wound inflicted to his thigh by the priest's pistol shot.

The guerrilla next to the wounded man leveled his rifle at the priest. Seeing the rebel's intention, Ramero dropped behind the wall, where the slugs crashed harmlessly into the stone.

Ramero turned to encourage Jose, but the villager was nowhere to be seen.

The priest glanced in both directions along the now-empty wall, then looked toward the village. There was Jose rushing into the hamlet, rebel bullets licking the dust at his heels, narrowly missing him as he jumped behind a stone hut.

Looks like the priest has been left to do the fighting, the cleric thought grimly, the black humor of the situation mildly amusing him. *So be it.*

He knelt behind the wall and prepared to empty his pistol at the oncoming gunmen.

20

"I don't think it's the Doppler inertial navigation system," Death Song said, inspecting the navigational reference points that were being updated on his screen by the 1750A/J73 dual mission computers.

"Let's check the SGPS," Oz suggested, bringing the chopper into a hover above the rocky hilltop where—according to their instruments—the village was supposed to be. While Death Song had locked onto the satellite global positioning system before they'd left Lima, it appeared their guidance system was in error.

"Luger," the pilot said, "give Dr. Lloyd a headset and see if he can help determine where we are. According to our data cartridge, this is the location of the village—and obviously it isn't here."

"Yes, sir," the young gunner answered, unclipping his seat belt and standing up.

"The computer's interrogating the SGPS now," Death Song told the pilot. "Downloading position update. And . . . according to global navigation sats we're right on the money."

Oz swore under his breath. "It's got to be the

maps then," he said, exasperated that the data cartridge they'd fed into the on-board computers was apparently in error. He realized that such faults were to be expected in areas that weren't heavily traveled and only cursorily surveyed; but such mistakes were still frustrating when they occurred.

"How can I be of help?" Lloyd's voice called over the intercom.

"We seem to be lost," Oz admitted. "Our maps show Piton as being right here, but obviously it isn't."

"Lost?" Lloyd said, rising from his seat and crossing to the side door to squint through the plexiglas window.

"Thanks to our instruments," Death Song quipped, "we know exactly where we are to within one foot."

"Yeah," Oz agreed, looking at his co-pilot knowingly, "we know *precisely* where we are—it's your village that's lost."

Lloyd chuckled. "I have to admit it's a little hard figuring out where we are from up here. I bet I've been over this ground a hundred times, but I don't recognize it. Let me check with my right-hand man."

The geologist pulled off the headset and turned to Espinoza. "Come here and see if you can recognize where we are," he called in Spanish.

Flashing his toothless grin, the villager staggered out of his seat and crowded to the door next to Lloyd, gazing from its window for a moment.

"Recognize anything?" Lloyd asked the peasant.

"Si," he answered, pointing with a gnarled finger. "Below us is *Simulado,* the false one. My brother and I once spent the night there because we thought we had journeyed to our village, only we hadn't."

"Where's Piton from here?"

"Over that way, across the ridge. About four kilometers, I think."

Lloyd put the intercom headset back on. "Captain, Espinoza recognizes where we are. He says Piton is about three miles to the east."

"Great. Get buckled back in and we'll be there in a couple of minutes."

"Sounds good," Lloyd said, handing the headset back to Luger.

The geologist and the villager settled back into their canvas and aluminum seats and buckled their shoulder harnesses.

"I'm going to be glad to get there," Lloyd hollered to Addison over the noise of the helicopter's engines. The arms merchant, seated next to him, smiled and leaned over to speak into the geologist's ear to make himself heard. "I know what you mean. My sitter's about sat out, too. I've heard the army designed these chairs so the grunts would be glad to exit—even if they land in the middle of a fire fight."

"I'd say they exceeded the design specs," Lloyd laughed.

Zurita lay on an improvised litter constructed of two ponchos and four AKMs, bound together with cord. The men carrying him strained mightily to haul the leader, carefully negotiating the rough trail that climbed steadily upward as they left the foothills and proceeded toward Piton.

The prone revolutionary felt humiliated that he

was forced to be carried like an old man. But he'd finally relented, finding it impossible to maintain the pace necessary to beat the government soldiers traveling from Lima to Piton.

As he bumped along the trail now, Zurita tried to save his strength the best he could.

"Comrade Zurita?"

"Yes," the rebel leader answered, his eyes blinking open. Though the sky was overcast, it was still bright enough to render it impossible to see the litter bearer who was speaking. Zurita closed his eyes and tried to recall the man's name.

Yannera, he finally remembered—one of the young men who had recently joined the group. "What do you need, Yannera?"

"To tell you it's an honor," the young man answered.

"An honor?"

"Yes, comrade. To carry you."

"Then you have an odd sense of honor," the rebel leader smiled, leaning back into the stretcher.

"No. I have heard how you carried one of your wounded comrades to safety following the attack on Pucallpa."

"That's history. That probably happened before you were born. We had to do things then that I'd be unable to do now."

"The stories we've heard about you!" Yannera continued. "Like the time—"

"The stories are greatly exaggerated, I assure you," Zurita interrupted, feeling uncomfortable with the young man's hero worship. "I'm simply a man who does what must be done. Just like you will. Do your best and you'll do better than I've done."

"I will try," Yannera pledged.

"Good. Now if you'll excuse me, I'm going to try to get rested so I can take part when we reach Piton."

"I will quit bothering you," Yannera said.

"No bother," Zurita answered, feeling suddenly old as he remembered a similar conversation he'd once had with one of his superiors, many years before. *And he is dead now,* the rebel leader told himself. There were few old men working in the Shining Path movement.

Zurita pondered his future as the litter rocked him back and forth; he'd come awfully close to death facing the Americans. Was this to be his last mission? he wondered. Contemplating the question, he was lulled into a deep, dreamless sleep.

21

"My God!" Lloyd cried from the passenger compartment, staring through the side window. "They're destroying my village."

"Sit down," O.T. called to the geologist through the open passageway that connected the two compartments. "We're going in to take the attackers. Everyone, be sure your harnesses are fastened good and tight."

In the cockpit of the MH-60K, Oz pushed the collective pitch lever downward, bouncing the chopper off the air reflected from the ground as they skimmed the rocky slope leading toward Piton. "Arm our weapons," he ordered his co-pilot.

Death Song snapped the switches to activate the armament. "Weapons armed."

Oz lifted the chopper and threw the collective pitch lever forward, inducing the nose of the MH-60K to dip the moment he throttled the fire button on the control column. The twin guns in the pod to the right of the chopper rattled, spewing empty casings earthward as the aircraft hurtled over the clump of rebels bathed by the spray of bullets.

Who was the lone figure trying to repel the guerrillas? Oz wondered briefly as they passed. It looked like a priest. The pilot cleared his mind and released the firing button, satisfied to see the rebel charge break up as the American chopper flashed overhead. He kicked the right rudder pedal slightly and threw the control column toward starboard, directing the chopper to circle the hamlet below.

Small arms fire from the ground rattled against the underside of the chopper with little effect; but the same could not be said of the bullets unleashed from the thundering Miniguns on either side of the MH-60K. Luger and O.T. riddled the rebels charging the village, slicing into the men who neared the stone huts at the western edge of the village.

As the chopper passed overhead, Oz could see villagers running to the outskirts, encouraged by the presence of the helicopter. He watched as they lifted a motley array of weapons and fired at the baffled rebels; one resident simply threw stones at the guerrillas.

"Mortar position at ten o'clock," Death Song declared.

The pilot scanned the area and altered their course, chasing toward a single mortar located on the nearby hillside opposite the village.

Jerking the chopper to the left to align it with the new target, Oz double-tapped the red button on the control column. Two folding-fin, 70mm rockets leaped from their 12-pack pod, hissing on flames as they streaked toward the target.

The four rebels manning the emplacement leaped away from the mortar but were too late to avoid the rockets.

The first missile struck just ahead of the emplacement, bowling over the men and their weapon in a cloud of dirt and rock. The second warhead exploded beneath the airborne men, ripping them to bits in a fiery explosion, the fury of which increased with the detonation of the mortars surrounding the position.

As the chopper raced through the shower of dirt above the explosion, Oz shoved the control column to starboard, kicking a rudder pedal to flip them around. Then he slammed the control column forward, sending them speeding onto a new course heading that would intersect with the remaining band of guerrillas.

The rebels were still advancing on the eastern slope of the village when the pilot lowered the collective pitch lever and dropped the MH-60K to follow the rolling landscape below. O.T. and Luger commenced firing at remnants of the band as the helicopter leaped the hill.

Oz again lifted the chopper with a tug on the collective pitch lever and jabbed the control column forward, his machine guns blazing. This time he aimed low so his bullets ricochetted through the crowded rebels, many of whom froze in fear as he hurtled toward them.

By the time he abruptly ceased firing to avoid hitting innocent citizens, most of the rebels had been downed. Several of the villagers waved and shouted in the streets as the American helicopter darted overhead.

"The rebels are turning tail and heading back down the slope," O.T. announced as Oz threw the chopper into a tight circuit of the village.

"See if you can ace the last of them," the pilot called to the gunners, shoving the control column forward to follow the fleeing attackers. He crossed above them, then slowed to a near hover to circumvent their escape route.

O.T. and Luger punched ten-shot strings from their Miniguns, raining a deadly salvo onto the last of the rebels, who futilely aimed their rifles at the advancing chopper. The six-barreled guns blurred, sending their fatal fusillade earthward, piercing the last of the attackers.

The thunder from the Miniguns ceased.

"That's all of them," O.T. said somberly.

The pilot rotated his fighting machine above the slope for a final inspection of the carnage. For a brief instant Oz almost felt remorse for the broken bodies littering the hillside below. Then he remembered Lloyd's story about the children in the schoolroom.

His face expressionless, he banked the chopper toward the village. "Let's head back and see what we can do to help the injured," he said. "O.T., go back and tell the *Cinchis* medic he'll have more than enough to keep him busy for a while. And tell Addison and Conrad to get their super-guns erected ASAP at the edges of the village."

"Will do," O.T. answered.

As he eased the chopper above the open square at the center of the village, Oz faced the helicopter into the wind and lowered the collective pitch lever, increasing his right rubber pedal pressure to keep the nose of the MH-60K toward the right heading. Hovering just above the ground, he hit the cargo hook release button on the control column.

He shoved the control column to starboard and lowered it to the ground, depressing the right pedal to keep the nose pointing into the wind. As the ground cushion effect kicked in, the pilot pushed the collective pitch lever down, squinting in the cloud of dust raised by the rotors. The landing gear touched the earth, and he swiftly cut the throttle. "O.T. and Luger, jump out and keep the villagers clear of the tail rotor."

"Will do, captain."

Oz studied the awed villagers gathering around the square and wondered what was in store for them when the Shining Path learned about the discovery of gold in Piton.

C H A P T E R

22

Father Ramero, Lloyd, and Oz worked side by side as they helped dig through what was left of the village school. A mortar had landed on its roof, inflicting severe damage to the one-room structure.

"I have to admit, I was astonished when I observed you fighting the rebels," the pilot told Ramero as the two pulled away the heavy front door of the school.

Lloyd flashed a smile. "I think Father Ramero would raise a few hackles in the cathedral at Lima if they knew how he helps protect his flock."

The priest bent down and peered into the rubble-filled interior of the school. "And why is it that everyone thinks those of the faith should lie down and play dead at the first sign of trouble?" he asked in heavily accented English.

"I'm not sure," the pilot admitted.

"I've always heard about turning the other cheek," Lloyd told the cleric. " 'Thou shalt not kill' and stuff like that. How *do* you get around those teachings?"

Father Ramero smiled. "You two must be Protestants. 'Get around teachings'—indeed."

"I'm not really anything," Oz answered. "Bedside Baptist, maybe."

"Pardon?" the priest queried.

"I stay in bed when the Baptists hold their meetings," Oz deadpanned.

"We have a few of your faith here in the village," Ramero grinned.

"I don't think we should try to go in there," Lloyd interjected. "It looks like that roof could collapse any minute."

"We're fortunate the school was empty when they attacked," Father Ramero said, glancing at the broken tiles on the tilted roof.

Lloyd paced to one side of the building and returned to the original subject. "I guess I relinquished my religious beliefs when I learned about evolution," he remarked.

"God preserve us," the priest muttered, only half in jest. "As to the scriptures you were half-quoting to me a moment ago, this is one of the problems with the do-it-yourself religion most Protestants engage in. Sometimes it's good to have a little professional help."

"I don't think I follow you there," Lloyd said, stopping to inspect the interior of the school through the open window.

Ramero explained. "One of the tenets of Protestantism is that every man can interpret the Bible for himself," he said, grunting as he lifted a stone, then turning to face Lloyd. "The translation of the Bible into German and English fueled the Protestant Reformation and changed the church in Rome as well. But those old translations weren't always perfect. The 'thou shalt not kill' of the King James, for example, should be 'thou shalt not murder.' There's quite a difference. Find a new translation sometime and check."

"So *that's* why the Hebrews could still be obeying the Ten Commandments while they were stomping the people living in the Promised Land," Lloyd said, more to himself than the others. He helped Oz pull away a huge stone, then rolled it into a pile of rocks outside the front door of the school.

"So you're saying it's all right to kill a foe in battle according to how you read the Bible?" Oz asked.

"Provided the battle you fight is just," the priest answered, bending over to peer through the hole the two men had created in the wall of the school.

Oz pointed toward the top of the building. "We could use the chopper to lift that heavy rafter out of the rubble. It looks like it's ready to fall."

"That'd help," Lloyd nodded.

"But our first concern had better be repairing the perimeter wall around the village," Ramero told them. "I'm afraid we haven't heard the last from the Shining Path."

"I think you're right on that one," the geologist agreed.

"Maybe we could kill two birds with one stone—or one beam in this case," Oz said. "We could use our chopper to lift the broken rafter, along with some larger rocks, and drop them into the breach in the wall down below us."

"That'd sure get the perimeter into shape faster," Lloyd agreed, glancing at the priest, who nodded. "We're game if you are."

"Let me round up my crew," Oz said, clapping the dirt from his hands.

Oz lifted the MH-60K into the air to complete its final workhorse run over the village, a heavy beam dangling on the cargo hook below. The pilot rapidly ferried the cracked beam to the wall where the *Cinchis* and the villagers were working side by side to make the barrier as impregnable as possible.

The pilot glanced to the east slope where Addison and Conrad were deploying the last of the four Osbourn-Newport XG-223 self-firing machine guns. The units looked like giant bugs, with a Gatling and a radar dish mounted on their backs. Spindly legs with stake-like feet extended from the mechanisms of the weapons to keep them steady on the ground.

As the chopper passed overhead, Conrad punched the proper code into the lock on the armored weapon, and a foot-wide door beeped open to reveal the computer's keyboard and liquid crystal display screen. "Shall we set this one on max, too?" he asked his partner.

Addison stared over the open hill below them. "Yeah, might as well," he answered. "Looks like there could easily be targets clear out to 800 meters. We should be able to just barely overlap the fields of fire."

"Sucker program again?"

"Of course," Addison retorted. The sucker program allowed intruders to advance to within 500 meters before the weapon initiated its attack, rather than hitting potential targets at the weapon's extreme range. Once more of the targets crossed the 500-

meter point, the XG-223 commenced firing, striking
every target it had recorded in its memory until everything within its 800-meter maximum range had been
neutralized.

"This air is so invigorating up here," Addison
said, unconsciously rubbing his hands together.

Conrad keyed in the perimeter orders to the
unit's computer, carefully shoving at the unit to verify
that it was stationary, and then punched in the final
commands for the unit. "It's hard to believe these
might be firing at live targets for a change," he mar-
veled.

"Yeah, I hope some of those jackasses attack tonight," Addison said. "If they do, they'll get one hell
of a surprise, won't they?"

"That does it," Conrad announced, stepping
away from the automatic gun. "Want to help with the
honors?"

"Sure," Addison replied.

He and Conrad picked up six large rocks from
the hillside.

"Ready?" Addison asked, cocking his arm. "On
three. One, two, three."

The two hurled the stones in different directions
so they dropped into the area covered by the XG-
223's radar.

In a blur of motion the machine snapped to life,
locking onto each stone and beeping loudly, but not
yet firing at the targets. After tracking each of the projectiles in the air, the weapon then swiveled around
and beeped at each of the stones again as they rolled
along the ground.

Only when all movement on the ridge had ceased did the servos whirl the gun into its neutral position.

"Fantastic!" Addison said. "Every time I see that thing do that, I get goosebumps. You've got the remote locked in?"

"Yeah," Conrad answered, holding up the black radio control that looked like the remote control for a TV set. "All four of the units are keyed to it now. Push the arming button from anywhere in the village and they're ready to fire."

"Fantastic," his partner muttered again, giving the XG-223 a pat before turning to follow Conrad down the ridge to the village.

"So where's the gold you found?" Sergeant Roque Luis pumped Lloyd as the American chopper hovered above, lowering the broken beam into position.

"It's well hidden," the geologist answered, shoving against the beam to swing it into line. "We're not going to reveal its location until the mining people get here from Lima."

"But surely you can trust me and my *Cinchis* squad," the soldier laughed. He pushed the beam with his shoulder to align it properly, then stepped back to wave at the chopper, signaling for it to drop its load. "Stand back!" he shouted at one of the villagers.

Observing everyone was clear of the beam, O.T. released the hook and the huge rafter groaned as its weight settled onto the wall.

"Now let's get the loose rubble piled in around it," Lloyd told the villagers. He wiped the sweat from his brow and turned to Sergeant Luis. "It's not that I don't trust you with the information about the gold. It's just that if the guerrillas capture you or your men, the less you know, the better."

Luis nodded, comprehending Lloyd's meaning. "You're right," he said, his face clouding over as he recalled the tortured soldiers he'd recovered from the Shining Path three years before. "The less we know about the gold, the better."

Lloyd turned and inspected the wall, squinting in the dust kicked up by the chopper's departure. "The wall's beginning to look like it might actually keep them out."

"The thorn bushes on the top are a good idea," Luis admitted, studying the long briars lining the top of the wall. "Too bad we don't have some cement to embed broken glass along the top."

"We save every bottle up around here anyway," the geologist said, bending over to position a huge stone into a space in the perimeter. "So you couldn't talk the villagers out of much glass even if you had the cement. All the containers are used for canning."

"I'm going to station my men at intervals around the wall," Luis said, helping to shove the stone into the gap. "If an attack occurs, the villagers can take positions along the wall. But they must understand that they are to stay out my men's way."

"I'll be sure they're told," Lloyd promised, straightening up and flexing his stiff spine. "Believe me, they're not too anxious for another skirmish. They'll be more than happy to let your soldiers do most of the fighting."

"I noticed the fresh graves in the cemetery," the

sergeant said. "I don't plan on any more of your people or mine being buried during the next few days. My men are seasoned troops. Don't worry, they'll be able to take care of ten times as many rebels."

"I'm hoping the four robots the Americans have installed at the corners of the village will do the job," Father Ramero commented, approaching the geologist and soldier.

"They may help," Luis admitted. "But I've never seen a real battle where it didn't get down to man against man."

"Then perhaps we'll see something new under the sun," the priest smiled.

23

Zurita wrote with a pencil stub, carefully drawing a map of Piton, working by memory from the three times he'd visited the village. After his long rest, he'd awakened stiff but feeling much better. Now that he was in his old camp, he felt renewed. *I feel like a leader again,* he thought.

"It will be dark in about three hours," he told the four men he'd designated to lead his forces. They sat around a crude table in the smoke-filled cave south of Piton where the rebels often hid during the day. "We'll meet at this hill by the village," he tapped the primitive map with his finger. "Then we'll wait until sunset and ascend in the darkness, although we still need to be careful of the American night vision devices. Once in the valley leading to Piton, we'll split into three groups—be sure your men remember which party they're in."

The four leaders reassured Zurita that their men would remember, while the revolutionary paused to take a cup of steaming coffee offered to him by one of the others.

Zurita resumed, his voice echoing off the cavern

walls. "Groups A and B will ascend the southern and eastern slopes, here and here," he indicated on the map. "In the past, the villagers have booby trapped these areas so you'll need to go slowly and cautiously."

"What happens if we run into a booby trap?" asked Miguel, leader of the southern attack.

"Then you'll probably blow off your foot—if you're lucky. But I'm giving each team leader a pair of the night-vision goggles that we captured from the *Guardia Civil*. If you're careful, you should be able to locate any of the traps and avoid them.

"If someone does run into a trap and alerts the sentries in Piton, you'll hold your positions and wait to commence firing on my orders after we get Team C and the mortars in position. There's no need for those in groups A and B to try to get any closer to the village since you're simply diversionary. Your job is to keep the villagers busy by making them believe the main attacks are coming from the south and west."

"What if we avoid the booby traps and get into the village without being detected?" Miguel inquired.

"That'd be great," Zurita replied.

Yannera chuckled at Miguel's optimism; but Zurita caught his eye and imperceptibly shook his head. Then he continued. "Remember that it's not essential that you get into the village—you're only diversionary. If you can get into Piton, then push as far as you are able and destroy as much as possible."

"I bet we can take the village before C gets into place," Miguel boasted, daring Yannera to laugh at him again.

"If you do, that would be a nice surprise for this

bag of bones leading you," Zurita remarked. "But this isn't a child's game, and I don't want to sustain a lot of casualties because various teams are competing to be first into the village. It's better to hang back if you run into strong resistance or large numbers of booby traps. Of course, the biggest danger is the American chopper."

"We've never had problems avoiding the choppers in the past," Miguel said.

"This chopper is different," Zurita countered. "It has weapons like you can't imagine: rockets and guns that fire from the front and both sides. But I think we can handle it by having some of our men work in tandem, firing our Redeyes and LAW-80s in pairs. I don't see how the pilot will be able to escape both. Even if he does, he'll be so busy countering our rockets, we'll have time to complete our mission before he can counterattack. Yannera, you've already been briefed on what I want your team to do with the missiles."

"Yes, comrade."

Zurita paused and took another sip from the mug of coffee. "Now here's what C will be doing while A and B divert the villagers' attention and Yannera's men handle the chopper."

"All four of the XG-223s are on-line, Captain Carson," Addison told the army pilot. "Anybody tries to approach the village tonight and they'll look like Swiss cheese."

"You're sure the weapons won't spend the night picking off rabbits?" O.T. queried, walking toward the church with the rest of the helicopter crew and the two sales representatives.

"Not unless they're carrying rifles," Addison replied with a chuckle. "The radar's set to target man-sized objects carrying metal."

"New computerized radar system," Conrad added.

"Our guns won't be firing at a child or any other unarmed person entering the area," Addison continued. "Unless somebody's packing a rifle or a pistol, they won't be in any danger."

Luger changed the subject. "What's this get-together we're headed for, captain?"

"The villagers are hosting a banquet for us," Oz replied, pulling open the door to the chapel. "They want to tell us thank you for saving the village from the rebel attack and for helping them clean up afterward."

Oz held the door open as the six Americans entered the chapel, the smell of spicy foods greeting their nostrils. The interior of the church was ablaze with candles, which covered the altar and adorned crude chandeliers hanging by cords from the vaulted stone ceiling. The villagers were dressed in their finest clothing and crowded around the crude tables and chairs brought from their homes to replace the pews that normally filled the space.

The tables were spread with steaming bowls of food highly seasoned with onions and hot peppers. Oz surveyed the tempting dishes of rice, potatoes, and bread, and realized he hadn't eaten since breakfast.

"Look at that," O.T. said, nodding toward a mouth-watering roast that glistened under a thick sauce, just waiting to be sliced and served.

Kettles of soups made of vegetables and barley

simmered at one end of the hall in a fireplace that took the chill out of the evening air.

"Welcome!" Father Ramero called to the visitors who stood at the entrance. "Come in and sit in our place of honor."

Oz and the others picked their way through the affable peasants to stand beside the priest. "Don't be afraid to eat the food," the cleric whispered to his guests. "The sister has taught the villagers the ins and outs of hygiene and food storage. I suspect the food's safer here than it is at your army base in the states."

"Kind of a left-handed compliment to your cooks," O.T. chuckled to himself.

"We'll start with our song of greeting and then a prayer," the cleric explained.

"Then everyone can dig in," Lloyd told the men, crowding in beside them, half dragging his beautiful wife, Maria, by the hand.

Ramero lifted his hands and the crowd hushed.

One of the women began the eerie song of greeting. The villagers quickly joined in, their voices leaping along the melody's odd tonal patterns. The bass voices of the men added an unearthly counterpoint, duplicating ancient harmony at least seven centuries old, written by a forgotten Aymaraian in the golden age of his lost culture. The song ended on a piercing note that reverberated from the stone walls.

Oz felt himself shiver, despite the warm coziness of the chapel.

The priest lifted his hands and everyone bowed to pray, the statues of the patron saints lining the walls looking on.

Before the cleric could speak, Oz's attention was

drawn to a soft, electrical beeping to his left. As the priest began his prayer, the pilot cautiously peeped at the Osbourn-Newport sales representatives who were whispering and studying the hand-held remote control linked by radio to their XG-223 guns.

One or more of the weapons must have detected something moving at the edge of the village, Oz thought. The question was whether it was something serious or just a malfunction of the experimental weapons. Since the American chopper crew had killed the last of the rebels who had attacked the village just hours before, it seemed unlikely that more guerrillas would already be in the area. Plus it looked like the two salesmen were unsure what to make of the signal. *It must be a malfunction,* the pilot decided.

The two salesmen continued their heated exchange in whispers that were inaudible under the priest's booming prayer. Finally their conversation ended and Conrad bowed his head, while Addison carefully picked his way through the Americans to stand next to Oz.

The moment the prayer ended, Addison leaned toward Oz and spoke. "I think we've got a problem, captain."

"Did your machines detect something?"

"Maybe. We're not sure. It looks like there are at least thirty men if the reading's right. But that many intruders so close to sunset after you and the villagers rubbed out the force attacking the Piton? I'm almost certain it's a malfunction of some kind."

"You'd better check your machines."

"Yes, sir. Immediately—if that's okay."

"Certainly," Oz said, puzzled as to why the sales

representative seemed to think he needed permission from 'the army officer to inspect his equipment.

"Let's not say anything to the villagers until we're sure," Addison said. "No need to upset them in the middle of their wingding."

"Okay," Oz replied. "But alert Sergeant Luis that something may be up so he can have his *Cinchis* keep watch just in case."

"Where is he?"

"He should be somewhere near the chopper in the empty hut where he's set up his command post."

"Yeah, I know where it is. We'll holler if there's any sign of intruders out there, but I'm betting on some kind of glitch. Maybe a temperature inversion coupled with the high percentage of metal ore in some of the rocks around here."

"Let us know what you find," Oz said.

The two sales representatives edged their way past the noisy crowd of villagers milling around the room, filling their clay plates from the large bowls of food. Oz was relieved to see that none of the native Americans seemed to notice the two departing salesmen.

The pilot turned back to the others.

"What's going on?" O.T. asked.

Oz quickly briefed them about the problems with the XG-223s. "Hopefully, it's a false alarm," he concluded.

"I don't know," the priest said. "I have a strange feeling about this."

"Are you still taking bets?" Luger quizzed O.T.

"Hey, this guy has an inside track with God," O.T. answered, nodding toward the priest. "All bets are off."

Conrad checked the XG-223 again. "It looks okay," he finally said. "The diagnostic program's coming up nominal. Is anybody out there?"

"No," Addison replied, lowering the night vision goggles so they hung from the strap that encircled his neck. He rubbed his tired eyes. "I don't see anything out there. Nothing."

"With all those boulders, I'm not sure you would unless someone was pretty obvious," Conrad said. "You could hide a herd of elephants on those hills and not be able to detect them from here."

"How far does the computer say they are from the 500-meter alarm?"

Conrad checked the display at the rear of the XG-223. "Supposedly, they're at 520 meters. Barely creeping forward—like they're crawling. Think we should take it off sucker mode?"

"No, if we're testing it, this is the time to leave it on."

"What have you got?" Sergeant Luis asked, approaching so quietly in the darkness that Addison jumped when he heard the soldier's voice.

"According to our machine there are thirty men out there," Addison replied irritably. "Twenty due south and ten more on the western slope."

"My men haven't seen any sign of intruders, even with their NVGs," Luis said, surveying the XG-223 with obvious distrust. "I thought this machine was supposed to fire if it detected somebody."

"Once they get to within 500 meters it starts firing," Addison answered. "That way they come into range so we can clean their clocks; anyone within 800 meters of us will be history once the machine starts firing."

The sergeant raised his eyebrows and shook his head. "I'll let you know if my men observe anything unusual."

"Thanks," Addison said. When the soldier was out of earshot, he confided his private sentiments to Conrad: "That Peruvian SOB doesn't think the equipment's working. I hate working with third-world hot shots."

Conrad glanced at his partner. "To be truthful I'm not so sure he isn't right. Hang on! One of the blips is almost at the alarm range—"

Abruptly the machine whipped to life with its whirring servo motors, firing down the ridge in a rapid staccato that rendered further speech impossible. The tracer rounds etched red lines into the darkness, the weapon pelting the two salesmen with empty brass as it locked onto various invisible targets.

Conrad hollered an oath and jumped away from the machine as it flashed to new aiming coordinates faster than the blink of an eye. The mechanic turned and stared at the weapon as if it were an animal gone berserk.

The XG-223 jerked belted ammunition from its hopper, jabbed it into chambers, and picked off targets so fast it was impossible to perceive anything besides a streak of motion.

Addison ignored the machine and watched the tracers.

The thing seemed to be firing according to its programing, he reflected. It didn't really look like it was malfunctioning: bullets were racing toward targets just like they had in the countless tests he'd conducted, hitting the extreme ranges first.

Then it rapidly re-aimed and fired, working its way forward to the closest targets, barrels coughing slugs and swiveling so quickly it was impossible to discern how the machine even operated. The thunderous ripping of nearly continuous discharges hurt the salesman's ears; even though Addison knew the weapon stopped momentarily for its computer to realign on new targets, he could discriminate no break since the computer re-targeted in just microseconds.

After what seemed like an endless pounding, the machine stopped, its six barrels smoking from the heat generated by the rounds. The smell of burnt paint and gunpowder hung in the crisp, evening air.

The two sales representatives stood transfixed.

Finally, Conrad broke the silence. "What in God's name just happened?" he said, talking more loudly than usual since his ears rang.

"Either we just witnessed one hell of a demonstration of what the XG-223 can do," Addison re-

sponded, "or we saw one crapola of a malfunction. I
wish I knew which."

"I guess we'll know tomorrow, if there's anybody
lying in the rocks out there," Conrad said.

"I'd sure like to know tonight," Addison responded, slowly realizing he was in a crouch. Straightening up, he instructed his partner to deactivate the
machines. "Let's go figure out what the hell's down
there."

"Wait a minute," Conrad protested. "We can't
just deactivate the machines and go wandering around
out there. What if there are rebels; we'd be on a live
battlefield just asking to be shot by anybody who survived. Besides, the machine on the western slope still
has readings that haven't come to within 500 meters
yet. And now the eastern slope's registering targets,
too."

Addison was quiet a moment and then spoke.
"We don't have to deactivate the guns at all with the
new FOF circuitry in place. We could just go on down
and—"

"The friend or foe program hasn't been fully
tested," Conrad protested. "There's no way I'm going
to—"

"But you said FOF is working perfectly," Addison countered. "The circuits will keep it from targeting us as long as we're unarmed; at the same time, the
machines can hit any rebels in the area, right?"

"That's a nice theory," Conrad retorted hotly,
"but you forget we're checking whether or not the
circuitry's screwed up. If it *is* malfunctioning, there's
no reason it won't do it again—and chew our asses off
while it's at it."

"I guess you're right," Addison admitted, embarrassed by the mistake. He thought a moment. "Well, how about this: we switch off the gun covering the southern slope and leave the others on. Then we go down and have a quick look-see. If there're bodies there, we know the machine's working and we can switch it back on to cover us while we hightail it back up here. If the machine's malfunctioning, we'll know *that* because no one will be down there."

"I don't like this idea any better than the others," Conrad declared.

"What's wrong with it?" Addison asked. "We can use our NVGs so we can see what we're doing. Hell, it'll be fun."

Conrad didn't answer immediately as he tried to weigh the merits of the idea.

Addison raised his night vision goggles to his eyes. "Come on, it'll be a chance to get the old adrenaline flowing without much risk. If we hurry up, we can get back before the villagers finish eating. Switch off this gun."

As Conrad hesitated, Sergeant Luis came charging up behind them, making no effort to be quiet as he approached. "What the hell's going on over here?" he demanded.

"Looks like a malfunction," Addison responded. "We're about to check it out. How about having your guys watch out for us from here?"

"If you go down that ridge, I can't promise that we can protect you," Luis stated. "In fact, I recommend that you stay behind the perimeter."

"I'm afraid you don't have any jurisdiction over us," Addison said evenly, climbing onto the top of the wall. "We're just going to be gone a few seconds, anyway."

Luis hesitated.

"We'll be right back," Conrad promised, lowering his NVGs over his eyes. He taped the deactivation switch on the remote control unit he held, then closed the instrument's cover and placed it in the pocket of his coveralls. "Sorry if we're messing you up," he told the soldier.

"Come on," Addison called from below.

Conrad turned and vaulted over the wall to descend the slope with his partner.

Luis watched the two Yankees, fuming at his inability to keep them inside the perimeters. Then he jerked the radio from his pocket to contact his men.

Things are bad enough without one of my soldiers firing at the Americans, he thought, *even if they do deserve to be shot.* "Attention," he barked into the transmitter. "We've got two Americans climbing down the south ridge. Do not fire at anyone in this area. Confirm message. Over."

"No, hold your positions," Zurita whispered into his radio to the platoon leader on the southern slope. "Do not retreat and do not return fire until we get into position. Sit tight until you receive further orders."

Satisfied that his platoon leader had finally calmed down, Zurita switched off the radio. *What could have done so much damage in such a short time?* he wondered dumbfoundedly. He'd heard the sound of the distant machine-gun fire as he and his group had climbed the eastern ridge; the burst was like rolling thunder echoing from a distant hill.

And the discharge had been continuous—the way untrained men fire machine guns: one long burst that continued until the ammunition in the weapon was exhausted. Yet Zurita's platoon leader claimed to have sustained massive casualties. *And Miguel reputedly never panicked in battle.*

Zurita swore quietly to himself and set his rifle's night-vision scope to its maximum setting. He lifted the viewer to study the crude wall ringing the village nearly 600 meters ahead.

There! He fastened his sight picture on the corner of the wall. That had to be one of the odd machines his platoon leader had described. Apparently one of the weapons was situated at the edge of the wall on this side of the town, too.

What is that thing? Zurita speculated, studying the spidery machine through the rifle's NSP-3 night vision sight.

The Yankee weapon—if that was what it was—was unmanned.

Can the Americans fire it by remote control? he wondered. He finally decided that it operated too quickly for that. And his nearly hysterical platoon leader on the southern ridge swore that the deadly weapon had targeted each of his men precisely, killing or wounding nearly every one of them.

It's impossible for one machine to do that in such a short period of time, the revolutionary reflected.

Acting on a hunch, he rotated his rifle and inspected the other corner of the village. One of the mechanical insects stood there, too, its barrels looking right at him.

So there must be four of the weapons, he realized, one on each corner, guarding the village like Incan death angels. *Is there any way to overcome such a machine?* he wondered, lowering his rifle.

An idea began to form in Zurita's mind. If he could quickly knock out the machines, it might be that the village would be left nearly unguarded. After all, who would post guards if they had the mechanical marvels the Americans had brought with them?

Zurita smiled at the idea that the Yankees' technological strength might be turned into a weakness. The trick would be in destroying at least one of the mechanical guardians and rapidly entering the village.

The LAW-80s might just do the job, he hypothesized.

Zurita gently set down his rifle, lifted his radio, and called Yannera.

The radio hissed to life. "Yes, comrade," the subordinate answered.

"Bring three of the LAW-80s to me at once."

"I'll be there in a moment, comrade."

Zurita pondered the changes he'd have to make for the attack to succeed. In just a few minutes Team C would be in position; the mortar crews were standing by.

He finally admitted to himself that the plan could work. It would take a little luck and a lot of daring on his part, but he was certain he could still successfully complete his mission.

25

"They *what?*" Oz demanded, placing his mouth right next to the radio speaker to make himself heard above the noise in the chapel.

Sergeant Luis repeated, "Conrad and Addison went down to see if the XG-223 had hit anything."

Oz swore under his breath and again thumbed the "voice" switch of the An/PR-4 radio. "Keep an eye on them and let me know if they run into trouble," he ordered Luis. "In the meantime, don't let anyone else go out. And when those two return, tell them I want to talk to them *immediately!*"

"Yes, sir."

The pilot left the radio antenna extended and set the transmitter on the table top in front of him.

Lloyd expertly cut another slice of roast with the razor-sharp Air SOG folding knife he carried in a belt pouch at the small of his back, speared the chunk of meat and stuck it into his mouth. "Having trouble outside, captain?" he inquired.

"I hope not," the pilot answered, picking up a piece of corn bread. "I wouldn't have thought that Addison and Conrad would be crazy enough to leave the village at night. As for their machine, it sounds like it went berserk and chewed up the whole southern slope."

"There's nothing that can be hurt down there," Ramero smiled. "All they can do is split the rocks into smaller pieces."

"Rocks are one resource we have plenty of," Lloyd agreed, impaling another slice of meat with his knife.

"All the same, I think I'll check with my superior tomorrow and see if we can't get the XG-223s deactivated," Oz replied, grasping a clay mug and sipping some Pepsi. O.T. had brought the soft drink as a gift for the villagers, who in turn had incorporated it into their banquet.

Oz was reminded of how different the lives of the Peruvians in the mountain hamlet were from his own, and he wondered if the gold would be a blessing or a curse for the people. Death Song had often spoken of the mixed blessings government-entitlement programs had been for his people.

"Well, don't be too hard on Conrad and Addison," Ramero said, breaking into Oz's reverie. "They were just trying to help the village."

"That's true," Lloyd agreed.

"When I was a kid in Virginia," Oz drawled, "my pa used to remind me and my brother that the primrose path to hell was paved with good intentions."

"An interesting thought," Ramero said, flashing the pilot an amused smile. However, as the evening wore on, Oz noticed that a distant expression kept returning to the cleric's countenance, causing the pilot to wonder if the priest, too, harbored some fears about the future of his people.

Conrad stumbled over a rock, falling to his knees with a loud oath.

"Shhh," Addison hissed. "You want to let everyone down here know exactly where we are?"

" 'Everyone'? There's no 'everyone' down here!" Conrad retorted irritably.

"We don't know that," Addison said. "Look, we aren't 500 meters from the perimeter yet. If there're any rebels, they'd be on down the slope a ways."

Conrad got to his feet, dusting off his already dirty coveralls. "I still say we should have waited 'til tomorrow. We have no business being out here in the middle of the night."

"You're probably right," Addison replied. "But we're here now so let's go see what the XG's shooting at."

They hiked twenty-seven yards down the hillside when Addison dropped to his knees. "Get down!" he whispered.

"What is it?"

"I saw something. Switch on the remote."

"Like hell I'm switching on the remote!" Conrad hissed. "I don't see anything down there. If I switch on that stupid machine and it's still malfunctioning, it could cut us to bits."

"No, I saw someone," Addison insisted, rising to his feet to peer into the darkness with his night vision goggles. He started to speak when a sonic crack snapped past him, the report of the rifle rumbling a hundred meters below.

"You see!" Addison snapped, collapsing to his knees to present less of a target. He turned toward his partner. "Now turn the damned—"

He stopped in mid-sentence, his eyes riveting on the cracked face of his partner. Addison turned and vomited. It was the first time he'd ever seen first-hand the results of a man being hit by a rifle bullet.

A second slug smashed into the rock next to him, its ricochet humming angrily in the darkness. *If I sit here I'm going to die, too,* he realized. Regaining his composure, he turned back to Conrad's body to search for the remote, avoiding looking directly at his partner's broken face.

There it is, he mumbled to himself, crawling toward the unit that lay in the gravel where it had dropped. He grabbed the unit and released its cover.

Another bullet cracked over his head. His finger jabbed at the arming button and he dropped to his face, waiting for the XG-223 to start its savage barrage on the slope.

But nothing happened.

Another bullet smashed into the rock next to Addison. Rolling onto his side, he examined the remote control. The back panel of the unit was split and the 9-volt transistor battery that powered the mechanism was missing, along with its cover.

Addison searched frantically in the gravel for the battery, then stopped cold when he detected the scraping of boots in the rocks below. The American jumped to his feet and commenced a mad dash up the hill toward the village.

A barrage of fire erupted from below. He managed to continue running even after a bullet had

smashed into his arm. A second projectile caught him
on the cheek, knocking out some teeth and filling his
mouth with blood.

He continued running.

A third bullet penetrated his back, exploding into
his heart. On he jogged, his arm flapping uselessly,
his chest burning, and his vision turning black as blood
gushed from the gaping wound in his back.

He proceeded another eight yards, took a final,
faltering step, and crumpled to the rocks.

Hearing the distant rifle reports, followed by the
distinctive pops of mortars leaving their tubes, Oz
glanced at O.T. and, at the same instant, both choked
out: "Incoming!"

There was a flurry of machine gun fire, then the
mortars exploded, rocking the church with their concussions. The villagers, recalling the previous damage
done by the mortars, instantly panicked, everyone
screaming and shoving their way toward the door at
the rear of the church.

Father Ramero snatched a child from the floor to
keep her from being trampled and begged for calm,
but his voice was lost in the bedlam.

"There's a rear exit," Lloyd screamed to Oz, unconsciously folding his knife and jamming it into his
belt pouch. "Follow me!"

The army pilot signaled his crew, and the four
American soldiers followed Lloyd as he strode to the
altar, half dragging Maria behind him. The crude
wooden door at the side of the sanctuary proved to
be stuck. Lloyd raised his booted foot and kicked the

planks, splintering the door apart as another barrage of mortars exploded in the air over the village.

After piling out the rear door behind the geologist and Maria, Oz turned and spoke loudly to his men. "Let's head for the chopper and see if we can get it into the air before it's hit by mortars."

"The XG-223s are intercepting the incoming shells!" O.T. hollered as they sprinted down the narrow street, weaving to avoid villagers with rifles charging to the perimeter walls to fight off the rebels. Oz glanced toward the east and heard another of the XG-223s rattling away. The mortars dropping toward the village were struck by the gun's bullets, exploding in the air with bright blasts that spilled light across the darkness.

So the experimental guns can neutralize mortars, Oz thought. *But how long before the XG-223s exhaust their ammunition?* When that happened, the village was going to be in for it, judging from the number of shells dropping out of the sky.

The pilot and his men raced around the corner of the narrow street and entered the unlit town square, where the MH-60K sat waiting in the shadows. Small arms fire was crackling from the south as the villagers assembled to fire down the slope, and the XG-223 on the western end of the village activated itself intermittently. *The rebels must be advancing from at least two sides,* Oz realized, ducking unconsciously as the angry whines of stray bullets passed overhead.

The Night Stalkers sprinted across the opening toward the helicopter as an explosion smashed one of the huts several doors away.

"The mortars," Death Song yelled, gasping for breath. "They're getting through."

Within moments the army flight crew had unlatched the doors to the MH-60K and piled in.

"Let's get it started!" Oz yelled, donning his helmet.

The pilot and navigator frantically completed the steps necessary for taking off, and within seconds the helicopter's twin engines sputtered to life. Oz adjusted the throttle, increasing the speed of the blades whipping overhead, then plugged his helmet cord into the intercom. "O.T., Luger, how are things back there?"

"Both aboard and standing by," O.T.'s voice crackled over the intercom.

The rotor overhead revolved to its proper rpm, kicking up a cloud of dust that surrounded the chopper. Another mortar landed fifty yards ahead of them, shattering a hut and pelting the skin of the MH-60K with rocks. Oz lifted the collective pitch lever and the chopper hovered a few feet off the ground.

Once in the air, the pilot kicked the rudder pedal, facing the helicopter into the wind to take advantage of the increased airspeed for a maximum performance takeoff. Then he boosted the throttle and raised the collective pitch, keeping the engine speed high so the rpms didn't subside while he eased the control column forward to propel the aircraft into the wind.

As the helicopter leaped skyward, Oz continued to increase the engine speed until he had a full throttle, altering the rudder pedals to keep them headed into the wind. "Arm our weapons," he ordered Death Song.

The pilot reduced his power and shoved the column to the side, throwing them into a roll above the village; Death Song flipped a series of switches. "Weapons are armed," he reported. "You have the machine gun and rockets; I've got the Hellfires."

Oz studied the FLIR a moment, then snapped a button along the edge of the screen, altering the picture to a negative of the first view. This provided the pilot a better picture of the terrain, due to the heat still retained by the mountain rocks. He pulled the chopper into a circle and sped around the village, gaining altitude as the four crewmen searched the area for enemy targets.

"Looks like the village is surrounded," O.T. said.

"Anybody see the mortars?" Oz asked. "We should go after those first if we can locate them."

"We've got radar locking onto us!" Death Song shouted.

Surely the rebels don't have radar, Oz thought. Then he realized what was happening. "The XG-223 must be locking onto us!" he exclaimed. "Death Song, activate our IFF."

"Squawk's on!" Death Song proclaimed. "But I've got a targeting signal now. Their gun isn't responding. Didn't the reps turn them off?"

There was a hammering on the underside of the chopper as hundreds of bullets smashed into the MH-60K, pummeling it with a heavy barrage. "Damn it!" Oz yelled, jerking the control column to the side. "Why isn't the gun recognizing the IFF signal?"

As the XG-223's blazing barrels continued to track them across the sky, the pilot anxiously speculated how long the armor on the underside of the helicopter could survive the savage beating.

26

"Ready to launch," Yannera yelled, the LAW-80 on his shoulder.

Zurita smiled grimly. The youngster handled the rocket like a pro. "Take out that weird gun on the wall," the leader directed, indicating the XG-223. "It keeps intercepting our mortars."

Yannera aimed, his fingers tightening on the launch lever.

Zurita turned back to watch the target and suddenly realized the spidery gun had locked onto the American helicopter. "No wait, don't—"

But it was too late.

The LAW-80 rocket exploded from the tube, the backblast hurting Zurita's ears as it kicked the projectile from the launcher. A moment later, the secondary rocket ignited, tearing toward the XG-223 at the edge of the village.

Zurita watched helplessly as the hi-tech weapon peppered the chopper for two more seconds. *Perhaps the rocket will miss,* he hoped ardently. Surely the intense fire would eventually damage the chopper, if it hadn't already. *Miss!* the rebel leader commanded the rocket.

The warhead connected. The XG-223 exploded in a bright blast, its ammunition detonating in secondary explosions spreading from the fireball.

Zurita closed his eyes and shook his head. *What rotten luck!*

"I hit it!" Yannera cried enthusiastically. "Now the way is clear for us to storm the wall."

The rebel leader was quiet for a moment. When he spoke, his voice was calm as he watched the American helicopter vanish into the darkness. "That was a fine shot, Yannera." *If only you hadn't learned to operate the LAW-80 so well,* he thought to himself. "Now go and get your teams prepared to deal with the American aircraft," he said to the boy.

The revolutionary leader lifted his radio and thumbed it on. "Groups A, B, and C, keep advancing as far as you can toward the village," he ordered. "Group C will hold its fire until we get to within twenty-five meters of the eastern wall. Mortar teams, keep the rounds coming; Piton's defensive guns seem to have exhausted their ammunition, so your shells are getting through now."

Zurita turned and followed Group C toward the village.

In the rocks ahead of him, his men stirred and stole toward the eastern wall of Piton with their leader, their guns silent to avoid detection.

Sergeant Luis ignored the helicopter that climbed above him and the mortars that plunged into the village. He concentrated instead on stopping the rebels ascending the southern slope directly in front of him. A burst of bullets glanced off the wall next to him, splattering him with bits of grit and cutting his temple. The Peruvian ignored the pain and raised his AKR, taking quick aim at one of the rebels puffing up the steep slope; the soldier's finger tightened on the trigger and the rifle fired, stopping the rebel cold.

Although the guerrillas were being cut to ribbons, Luis realized, they persisted in their assault. As he aimed and fired again, he wished his men would demonstrate that kind of determination.

He turned to one of his soldiers. "Get the RPK in place!" he yelled. The trooper fumbled with the weapon, a wound on his hand making it nearly impossible to deploy its bipod.

"Sergeant," the radio on Luis's belt sputtered to life.

Luis lifted the transmitter, surprised he could hear over the reports of the villagers' guns to either side of him. He tapped the transmit button on the AN/PRT-4 radio. "What is it?" he demanded.

"The rebels have nearly breached the western perimeter," the subordinate informed him.

"Do your best. I'll transfer some of the villagers to you, but be ready to fall back into the village to regroup. Over."

"Yes, sir."

"Over and out," Luis called, replacing the radio in the pouch on his combat suspenders. The soldier next to him had finally managed to get the RPK-74 in place, and when the gun started its high-pitched thumping, it drowned out the reports of the .22 rifles used by most of the villagers.

Luis turned to locate the few townspeople with AKMs, to send them to the other side of the village. As he crouched along the wall, an incoming mortar landed nearly on top of him and exploded, leaving only a smoking smear to mark where he had been.

"Several mortar crews at eleven o'clock!" Death Song yelled. "Check my FLIR."

Oz glanced at the forward-looking infrared scope which was locked to Death Song's helmet sensors. Although the enemy crews were nearly hidden, the hot tubes of their mortars glowed brightly on the FLIR screen, like beacons against the cooler background of the mountain rocks.

"Take them with the Hellfires," Oz ordered.

Death Song kept his head toward the target, holding the laser designator slaved to the FLIR on target. Using the tiny viewscreen over his right eye to align onto one of the mortar crews, he tapped the designator control, flashing a nearly invisible beam from the laser.

As the Hellfire locked onto the backscatter from the laser target acquisition and designation sight, Death Song launched the missile. The rocket flashed away from its pylon with a vociferous blast, ripping through the night and leaving a fiery after-image in the crewman's eyes.

Even after the laser winked off, the autopilot electronics at the center of the missile kept it on target, guiding it precisely to the designated spot. Death Song ignored the first rocket and shifted his vision to the side, ready to mark another of the mortar crews; the FLIR screen aligned itself onto the rebel gunners below and the co-pilot punched the designator. When the Hellfire signaled its laser seeker was on target, he launched the weapon.

"Enemy rocket!" O.T. yelled from the back as the second Hellfire tore away from the helicopter. "Five o'clock and closing fast."

Oz threw the chopper into a steep banking turn and dropped it toward the ground, quickly glancing over his shoulder to try to catch a glimpse of the enemy missile.

As the two Hellfires reached their targets, all five of the mortars and their crews disappeared in the furious fireballs and secondary explosions that enveloped the area.

Death Song shoved the Hellfire controls away from him and tapped a button on the countermeasure module to launch an infrared flare from its pod. The module's counter changed indicating that the stores had been depleted as the flare sputtered to life behind them.

The co-pilot then initiated the IR jammer aft of the main rotor above the engine housing; the device sent infrared signals that modulated up and down in frequency, making it more difficult for a missile to lock onto the heat coming from the dual engine.

"Second missile launch," Luger warned, hanging in his shoulder strap while the chopper continued to plummet toward the earth.

As Oz jerked the chopper onto a new course, the Redeye II behind them homed in on the flare and exploded.

Smashed into his seat by the now-climbing chopper, Death Song ejected another flare.

"The second one looks like a TOW or maybe a LAW," O.T. warned, leaning out his window. "It's moving pretty slow." He fired a burst from his Minigun at the missile's launch site in an effort to distract the person on the ground who guided the missile. "It's not compensating for our turn," he called, releasing the trigger on his six-barreled gun. "Must be a LAW."

The rocket passed by harmlessly, far to port.

Oz had just relaxed slightly for a moment when Luger suddenly erupted. "Two more rockets at four o'clock!" he shouted.

Oz selected a new course heading, accelerating away from the source of the missiles, as Death Song ejected another flare.

Whoever's firing the missiles isn't too skilled, Oz reflected gratefully as another of the projectiles exploded on the flare and its companion sped by harmlessly. But they were succeeding in keeping the chopper away from the battlefield, and that, the pilot realized, might be their sole purpose. "O.T., can you see where those missiles are coming from?"

"Yeah, about a thousand meters east of the village, near that spire."

"Got it," Death Song yelled as two more of the rockets were launched, their heat signatures clearly visible in the FLIR. "Another pair coming from the rock formation."

"Let's shake these two and see if we can get these guys before they get us," Oz said, guiding them into a steep bank as O.T.'s Minigun clattered at the distant launch site.

*   *   *

As Lloyd fired at the short rebel who leaped over the edge of the eastern wall, the American's M100 cut a bloody hole in the guerrilla's chest.

I knew they'd try to come over this wall while they distracted everyone on the other two, Lloyd thought, inspecting the perimeter for more insurgents. They'd used the same tactics before.

There! The geologist observed a rebel's eyes flickering in the firelight from the huts behind Lloyd. As the guerrilla peeped over the wall, Lloyd swung his rifle and fired, pumping the trigger three times.

The .22 slugs glanced off the stone, causing the guerrilla to run—either frightened, injured or both; the geologist couldn't tell.

"We need reinforcements over here!" Lloyd shouted over his shoulder. Nearly all the villagers had responded to the fighting at the south or west perimeters of the village, leaving the eastern end of Piton virtually unguarded.

A third rebel jumped the barrier, his gun blazing wildly, killing one of the few villagers who remained on the wall about twenty yards north of the geologist. The American pulled the trigger of his weapon and—realizing he'd exhausted the 100-round magazine—charged the guerrilla, smashing the barrel of his Calico against the man's skull.

The rebel staggered back, stunned by the blow. As Lloyd cuffed him again with his lightweight rifle, he shattered the weapon's plastic handguard and bent the barrel with the force of his attack. The American chucked the broken gun, grabbed the dazed rebel, lifted him overhead and threw him over the wall to the rocks below.

Then he bent over and scooped up the rebel's weapon, shouldered it, and fired at another of the insurgents who was approaching the perimeter. The slug ripped into the man's thigh, dropping him to his knees. Lloyd took aim at another guerrilla, barely distinguishable in the darkness; as the man crumpled up and rolled into the shadows, the geologist realized they were all over the hill.

Although Lloyd could see nothing, he could hear the clanking of metal and rocks being kicked aside by running men.

Finally, he spotted five rebels dashing toward the wall; as they boosted themselves onto a large boulder that jutted toward the top of the stone perimeter, Lloyd snapped the AKM's selector to automatic and fired a long burst, his gun transversing the men with bullets. The rebels writhed in pain and foundered into a tangle of limbs and weapons.

Lloyd discarded the empty rifle and looked around for something to replace it with. Observing the villager who'd fallen twenty yards from him, the geologist went dashing toward the body lying in the shadows.

The flash of a nearby mortar illuminated the man's face as Lloyd knelt beside him. "Jose!" he exclaimed. The geologist felt for a pulse at the villager's neck. He was dead.

Lloyd shook his head sadly and pried the pump shotgun out of the man's hands. Standing, he cycled a shell into the weapon's chamber and, hearing footsteps behind him, whirled around.

One of the *Cinchis* ran along the perimeter toward him.

"Come on!" the soldier yelled. "You must get back. They're going to be all over us in a moment. Look down the ridge."

Lloyd glanced to the east where the trooper pointed. At first he could discern nothing; then he was startled to observe at least forty of the rebels charging through the shadows toward the wall, their rifles at the ready.

"Radio your sergeant and tell him what's happening!" Lloyd demanded. "We need reinforcements."

"I tried already!" the soldier hollered. "He won't answer. We *must* retreat."

Lloyd yelled in Aymaran to the two remaining villagers on the wall some sixty feet away. "Fall back!" he ordered. "Retreat!"

Without warning, the line of Shining Path rebels below fired a withering barrage at the four men along the wall. The two villagers fell, either wounded or dead.

The geologist fired one final shot as the rebels rushed the wall, then discarded his now-empty shotgun. Turning to retreat, he nearly stumbled over Jose's body. He leaped the corpse and chased up the ridge, only slowing down momentarily when he saw a dark form lying on the ground ahead of him.

The American stooped over and picked up the moaning woman, slinging her over his shoulder. As he started to sprint up the ridge toward the safety of the stone huts, he turned to see how close the rebels were and a single slug caught him on the temple. The blow of the projectile caused the night to seem to light up around him.

Lloyd spilled onto the ground, the woman he carried falling into a tangle beside him. He struggled to rise, then fell again, limp and unconscious.

27

"Let's nail these bastards to the wall!" Oz exclaimed, dropping the chopper lower so the rocks on the surface raced below the belly of the MH-60K. He pushed the control column forward, increased their speed, and rapidly weaved through the boulders and hills blocking their path.

"There they are," Death Song warned.

Both the pilot and the co-pilot fell silent, concentrating on their weapons.

Oz launched eight rockets in a serial pattern, the Hydra 70 missiles flashing toward their targets; Death Song fired a pair of Hellfires at nearly the same moment. The ten rockets almost elbowed each other as they tore ahead of the chopper.

The blasts lit the sky with a brilliance that almost hurt the crewmen's eyes behind their night vision goggles. Seven of the warheads failed to strike any of the guerrilla-held Redeye II or LAW-80 missiles, but three of the rockets landed on the money, creating secondary explosions that increased the devastation to the area.

The pilot pulled on the collective pitch lever to

climb skyward, flashing over the scene of destruction. The smoke rising from the explosions was churned by the MH-60K's rotors into huge swirls that bellowed beneath them. As the chopper passed overhead, both O.T. and Luger fired their guns at the few rebels still standing.

"Looks like that took care of them," O.T. called.

"Keep a sharp lookout just the same," Oz warned. "They may have a few of those rockets squirreled away somewhere else." He jerked the chopper into a long banking turn, approaching the village from a low altitude.

Three large fires burned in Piton, and even from the air it was obvious many of the houses had been destroyed by the mortar and rocket attacks.

"I see several bands of men running away from the village," O.T. said over the intercom. "But I can't tell if they're guerrillas."

"Let's leave them alone, then," Oz said. "They probably are, but they might be villagers. It's better not to chance it. Try to keep track of their heading so we can scout them out later if we need to."

"We're getting something on the radio," Death Song said.

Oz clicked the radio on and heard the voice of Father Ramero.

"—calling the Night Stalkers."

"This is NS-1, we read you. Over."

"Oz, is that you?"

"That's a roger, but try not to use names over the radio. Over."

"Roger?"

"It's Oz. What have you got down there, Father?"

"The guerrillas have broken off their attack."

"Are any of the villagers outside the wall? If they aren't, we could take out some of the rebels from here."

"No, don't fire at anyone outside the wall," Ramero warned. "It looks like some of the villagers may be outside, or at least they're missing, maybe prisoners. Things are in a complete shambles down here."

"We're going to circle around to be sure another attack isn't being readied, then we'll come in. Over and out."

"Can I shut off the radio now?" Father Ramero asked.

"Yeah. We'll see you in a few minutes."

Oz circled Piton as he and his men searched the ground, failing to detect any of the bands of men they'd spotted earlier.

"It's like they fell off the face of the earth," Death Song said.

"I wonder if there're any old mines or caves in this area," Oz speculated. "We'll have to check with Lloyd when we get back to the village. There's no way they could have traveled beyond this point."

"And there's not enough vegetation to hide from the FLIR," Death Song added.

The rebels must have a hideout somewhere close by, Oz realized. If they could find it, they might be able to put an end to the attacks on the village once and for all.

He directed the helicopter toward Piton; smoke rose above the village, making it look like a smoldering volcano. The pilot dreaded landing in the hamlet, well aware of the carnage wrought by the rebels.

"Death Song and Luger, stay with the chopper in case we need to get it out of here in a hurry," Oz ordered, setting the chopper in the center of the village. "O.T., come with me. Let's see how bad things are so I can report back to Commander Warner."

"Yes, sir."

The two army fliers walked through a scene that, in terms of human suffering, reminded Oz of Vietnam. But the villagers were working to help each other. Women carried children to safety, men hauled the wounded toward the makeshift hospital in the church. Others dug through the rubble to rescue those trapped underneath.

"Captain Carson," Father Ramero cried, staggering across the street toward the two Americans. A cut above his eye had left a dark stain of dried blood across the side of his face.

"What can we do to help?" Oz asked.

"We seem to be handling everything," the priest answered, obviously close to shock as he viewed the disastrous condition of his village. "Right now we're concentrating on helping the wounded. But many of the villagers seem to be missing."

"I need to check with Lloyd to see if there are any caves or mines around here," Oz said.

"Lloyd and his wife are among the missing," the priest said. "With all the rubble around, it's possible they're trapped. Some of the villagers and one of the *Cinchis* also claim the rebels took prisoners when they stormed the east wall," the priest reported.

"Why would they take prisoners?" O.T. asked.

The priest shrugged. "Perhaps they want to make examples of them. The rebels act insane half the time, anyway—who knows why?"

"They might want to learn where the gold is," Oz suggested.

"Yes, of course that's it!" the priest exclaimed. "We've been keeping its location a secret, but the fact that we've found it seems to be spreading."

"Has anyone posted lookouts?" Oz asked.

"Yes, the six remaining *Cinchis* have been reorganizing our defenses," the priest answered. "But it seems so hopeless."

"Where's Sergeant Luis?" Oz asked.

The priest shook his head and began to weep.

"So that's about it," Oz explained over the satellite link to Commander Warner. "I have O.T., Luger, and Death Song helping the villagers, but there really isn't much we can do until daylight."

"Sit tight in the village," Warner ordered. "Don't search for the rebels—just stay on the defensive. We have three Apaches and two MH-60Ks headed your way but they aren't going to get into Lima for eight hours—and then another hour to Piton. In the meantime, I'm going to check with the guys in the big blue cube; they moved a K-11 over Lima for the vice-president's visit. They could be checking your area in no time."

"A satellite search might uncover something," Oz agreed.

"I'll also check with the Peruvians and find out if there're any abandoned mines in the area."

"Any word on the military convoy coming from Lima?"

"My latest info is it's still at least two days away. And the Peruvian military has its choppers tied up on the other side of the Andes southeast of you. So you're on your own until our 'copters come in to reinforce you."

"We'll sit tight and hope SIGINT gets something for us to go on. The sooner the better, though. I'd like to know if the rebels are massing for another attack."

"I'll contact you as soon as we get anything. Good luck. Over and out."

Hanging in geostationary orbit over Peru, the U.S. Signal Intelligence K-11 satellite altered its area of scrutiny to encompass the region surrounding Piton. The TRW-made instrument weighed 5,200 pounds and consisted of two distinct detection arrays.

A charge-coupled device similar to the sensor used in TV cameras comprised one section of the satellite. The solid-state CCD produced images of the region and was capable of spotting details as small as five inches across. The second detection array collected signals in the radio spectrum; it would intercept and transmit messages that might be sent by the rebels to contact various members of their organization.

The data from both sections of the man-made moon was digitalized and relayed to a tracking and data relay satellite system, which bounced the signals to the ground station located in Sunnyvale, California. There the information was received by the Onizuka Air Force Base antenna at the U.S. government's satellite control facility. Once on earth, the data was reconfigured, sifted by computers, and carefully analyzed for any clues to the whereabouts of the Shining Path rebels near Piton.

With mechanical precision, the satellite searched every square foot around the village, giving its analysts access to copious data about a few square miles of Peruvian rock and earth.

Two hours after the initiation of the satellite search, the super-sensitive lens had pierced the night to locate an odd pattern of rocks in a tiny grove of scrub bush and trees. An hour-and-forty-five minutes later, the photos were carefully surveyed by air force personnel, and the satellite was redirected to take a second series of detailed pictures of the valley. This surveillance revealed what appeared to be a camp complete with several crude tents and a camouflaged machine-gun nest.

The details of the find were immediately routed to Commander Warner who, several minutes after he had received the information via a scrambled phone line, uplinked to Oz on the COMSAT.

"I think we've located the rebels' camp," Warner told the pilot. "There's definitely a cave of some kind—we've got photos of people entering and leaving it. And some old Peruvian records seem to indicate there's an abandoned silver mine somewhere in the region—but there's no precise record as to where."

"We're missing some villagers here—including Harlan Lloyd," the pilot informed Warner. "I thought perhaps they'd been killed in the fighting, but they can't be accounted for. Are there any signs of prisoners in the photos?"

"A negative on that. There're people in the pictures, but it's impossible to tell what their status is."

"Any chance it could be a bunch of squatters?"

"No, there're weapons emplacements—I'll send the coordinates to you. And I double-checked to be sure the Peruvian military doesn't have anyone in there, either."

"What's the feeling on your end about our mounting a rescue operation?"

"Washington agrees with me that you should make the call on that. My thinking formerly was that you should wait, but the prisoner angle changes things. If we wait around, they'll likely either kill them or move them to another location."

"Yeah, that's about a given with the Shining Path," Oz agreed. He paused to think for a moment before continuing. "The *Cinchis* are out for blood; the death of their commanding officer seems to have become a point of honor with them. And the villagers are interested in doing anything necessary to get Lloyd back."

"How's your armament?"

"We still have half our rockets and can resupply our machine guns from the ammunition we brought; we can still pack quite a punch from the air. Plus we could take advantage of the four remaining hours of darkness if we left immediately. The *Cinchis* have NVGs and some of the villagers are good at operating at night, too. We could hit them hard with a surprise attack."

"You make it sound good, but it'd all be uphill," Warner cautioned.

"But they wouldn't be expecting us to hit them now," Oz argued.

"That's true. It's your call."

"I think we should go in, commander," Oz said. "We stand a good chance of getting the drop on them if we go ASAP rather than waiting for the Peruvian convoy or our own reinforcements."

"Okay. Get the *Cinchis* and any of the villagers you think might be able to handle the mission. Discuss it with them, then get back to me immediately so we can finalize plans. If you still think you can take the rebels, I'll give you the go ahead."

C H A P T E R

28

"You might as well tell me where the gold is now," Zurita informed the five prisoners at the back of the cavern, their arms and legs bound tightly so they could do little other than sit and glare at him. The darkness in the cave was broken only by a few flickering candles that cast long shadows on the walls and glistened off the rebel leader's dark eyes.

He paced back and forth in front of his restrained audience. "I'll get the truth from you sooner or later—but you won't live to tell about it if it's later," he warned.

"What good will the information do you now?" Lloyd asked. "You don't have enough men to take the village."

"I think you're mistaken there," Zurita replied, deciding there was no need to tell his prisoners more. *Once we know where the gold is, we might still take the village with the second contingent of fifty men that will be arriving here in hours.* The revolutionary had noted the villagers' weak resistance when his forces had stormed the eastern perimeter; another attack might enable them to take Piton—especially with the Peruvian military convoy still days away.

So there's still a chance I can complete my mission, he told himself. *If* he could find the location of the gold vein. "I'll release the first one of you who tells me where the gold is," he promised his captives.

"Like hell you will," Lloyd yelled. "You'll kill us all if you learn where the gold is."

"There's no reason to kill you."

"You can't risk having us tell about this hideout or the abandoned tunnel leading to the village," the geologist spit back at him.

Zurita drew his knife. While he did not relish torture, he realized it was going to be necessary to let the American geologist know he would stop at nothing to learn the truth. He held the razor-sharp blade in front of the American's face. "Perhaps you'd like for me to demonstrate what will happen if you continue to refuse?"

"You'll never know whether I'm telling the truth or lying," Lloyd said evenly, ignoring the sharp edge of the blade a half-inch from his brow. "If you're as familiar with torture as you seem to be, you know that men don't tell the truth, only what they think will stop the torture. I can lie through my teeth and you'll never know the difference."

"Perhaps this one can help us loosen your tongue," Zurita suggested, moving toward Maria, who sat trussed next to the geologist. "I've seen you staring at this woman when you thought no one was looking. Your wife? Or perhaps a lover? A white would probably never marry one with such dark skin."

Lloyd forced a laugh. "Nice idea but the wrong sex. I'm gay," he lied.

"Gay?" Zurita queried, turning to one of his men.

"Homosexual," Yannera whispered.

The American is trying to make a fool of me! Zurita thought angrily, turning with a savage thrust of his blade and aiming at Maria's face. She jerked her head back the instant he lunged at her.

"Quick little bitch," Zurita said with a laugh, seeing he had missed her. He turned back to the geologist. "I can see what she means to you by the expression on your face, Yankee. She's someone very dear. I'll give you twenty minutes to think about whether or not you wish to tell me your secret. Then if you choose not to speak, we'll start carving on her, then stake her to the large anthill outside. The ants come out at night; they'll enjoy the little treat." Zurita noted the change in expression on the American's face. "You could listen to her screams."

The rebel turned toward his men. "Bring her to the front of the cave with us. We'll let these four think about whether or not they wish to talk." He glared at the American. "You have twenty minutes. No more, no less. Then we'll begin to get serious—starting with your woman."

Lloyd watched the rebels drag his wife away. He strained at the ropes that bound him, renewing his efforts to reach the folding knife that the rebels had failed to notice hidden under his shirt tail.

The American chopper stormed through the murky night, headed for the rebel camp detected by the K-11. The helicopter hugged the earth, guided along the valley's floor by Oz's skillful hand. Their low altitude minimized the engine's noise, thereby reducing the chance of being overheard by the rebels.

"We're close to the SP, captain," Death Song cautioned.

Oz checked the horizontal situation display. The HSD showed a map projection and the navigation reference points updated by the 1750A/J73 dual mission computers. "I've got it," he told Death Song.

The TF/TA jacked them upward over the top of a bluff. Clearing the hill, they dropped downward again and followed a dry steam bed that had cut through the valley below.

"There's the LZ," Death Song announced, consulting his HSD.

The pilot bounced off the air pushed upward from the ground. He rotated the helicopter as it hovered to land across the slope, thereby preventing the tail from striking the hillside as they went in.

Oz slowly depressed the collective pitch lever until the port wheel touched the side of the incline, then shoved the control column toward the hill, anchoring the left landing gear against the slope. Continuing to lower the chopper, he pushed the control column farther to the left until he felt the other wheels touch down.

He turned to watch through the side window to be certain the rotors couldn't strike any rocks on the uphill side of the MH-60K. "Be sure no one exits from the port side, or they'll be looking for their scalp," Oz warned O.T. over the intercom.

"We'll keep the port door shut, captain," the warrant officer promised.

Luger slid the starboard-side door open and the troops and villagers jumped out. The fourteen men still wore the uniforms or clothing they'd had on during the battle with the rebels; dirty and unshaven, they carried a variety of weapons, including several machetes, two RPK-74 machine guns, AKRs, and silenced pistols.

The ragtag squad's strategy would be simple but dangerous: the villagers and *Cinchis* were to take out the two machine-gun nests overlooking the camp, then draw the rebels from the camp with an attack followed by a retreat. If the Shining Path contingent could be lured into the open to chase the squad, the *Cinchis* would radio Oz and the chopper would storm in to destroy the rebels.

"They're off," O.T. announced.

"Radio check," Oz called to Dagoberto, the *Cinchis* private in charge of the villagers and soldiers.

"I read you, NS-1," Dagoberto answered.

"Good luck, we'll come in when we get your signal."

Once the soldiers and villagers were clear of the chopper, Oz adjusted the throttle and shoved the control column to starboard, lifting the collective pitch lever to bring them into a hover. Having cleared the hill, the pilot kicked the rudder pedal to bring the MH-60K into its new heading, taking them in a circle around the rebel's hideout. This would allow the Americans to attack from the south if Dagoberto and his team succeeded in luring the rebels into the open.

*   *   *

"Captain, there're men down there," Luger called on the intercom. "At three o'clock. Forty, maybe fifty of them from the looks of it."

"Who in the world could be down there?" Oz asked.

"I see muzzle flashes," Death Song warned. "They're firing at us." As if to confirm what he'd said, a bullet slammed against the side door next to him.

"They're headed in the direction of the rebel camp," Oz said. "They must be teaming up with the contingent that attacked the village. If they get to the rebels before Dagoberto and the villagers—" He left the thought unfinished. "How far are we from the camp?" he asked, checking the VSD screen. "About four-and-a-half kilometers?"

"That's about it," Death Song agreed.

"They'll be at the rebel camp in no time, then," Oz said. That left little choice but to attack the new contingent of guerrillas below and hope the hills subdued the sounds of the American rockets and guns. If the air crew *didn't* deal with the rebels, the insurgents would be able to warn their comrades of the rescue operation.

"Arm our weapons," Oz ordered. "Let's try to get as many of them as possible—we don't have much time to spare."

"Quick and dirty," O.T. said.

"Quick and *very* dirty," Oz agreed.

The pilot banked hard to the right to circle back to the fifty rebels. "I'm going down the far end of the canyon they're in. If we can keep them boxed in, we might be able to take most of them."

"Our weapons are armed and I'm standing by

with the Hellfires," Death Song said. He glanced at the console where a red light was blinking. "Looks like we took some pretty good hits from the rebels a minute ago. Fifty-caliber gun, from the looks of it."

"Must be," Oz agreed since their armor stopped most smaller projectiles. He leveled the chopper and commenced their run, flying just yards above the rocky surface. "Death Song, if you see an HMG, make that your target. There're the rebels now."

"I see the guys with the machine gun," Death Song said, noting the bright flashes from the muzzle of the weapon.

"Fire at any target of opportunity when ready," Oz announced over the intercom.

The surface raced beneath the MH-60K, the rough terrain appearing green and white in the crew's night vision goggles. The pilot centered the nose of the chopper on the rebels ahead of him and launched a pair of 70mm rockets. He followed with his dual machine guns, aiming low so the strafing bullets would bounce along the rocks to hit more of the guerrillas.

The twin concussions of the rockets and the machine gun bullets killed or wounded thirty-two of the rebels where they stood. Those remaining on their feet either returned the Americans' fire or turned to flee toward the walls of the canyon that trapped them.

With his laser, Death Song designated the insurgents carrying the DShk38/46 heavy machine gun. The gun crew had persisted in firing the anti-aircraft weapon, but had failed to get its tripod deployed properly so the gun tracked poorly. Their shells streaked to the left of the chopper.

The Hellfire jetted away. The HMG crew finally

caught the MH-60K with a few of their rounds, the heavy 12.5mm bullets cutting through the armor of the chopper, causing the metal detector lights and fuel loss warning light to flash to life on the console.

The rebel machine gunners fired until the moment the missile struck, its fireball engulfing the weapon and the men, spewing bits of flesh and steel as it climbed upward in a fiery sphere.

The chopper flashed over the destroyed HMG, swirling the rising cloud of smoke and leaping over the last of the rebels. The helicopter's landing gear passed so low it missed the scalps of the screaming insurgents by only a few inches.

The two Miniguns on either side of the chopper erupted as the chopper passed overhead, the whine of the weapons' electric motors muffled by the explosion of burning gas and bullets from their six barrels. Both gunners aimed at the remaining rebels, who made no further effort to fight, trying now only to escape.

Oz lifted the MH-60K out of its run and banked.

"There're still a few left," O.T. called over the intercom.

"We don't have time for a second pass," Oz said. "I don't think they'll pose much of a threat. I'm hoping they'll stop to care for their wounded."

"Captain, we've got a problem," Death Song alerted the pilot. "We must've taken a hit from the HMG because we seem to be losing fuel."

Oz glanced at the warning light blinking on the console, surprised that the normally self-sealing fuel tanks could be leaking. "How fast are we losing it?"

Death Song punched a button alongside the

VSD, quizzing the computer for a readout. "It's going fast. The A tank will be dry in about three minutes. If it continues to leak, we'll only have ten minutes of flight time left before we're running on fumes."

The pilot tried to think of some way to stretch their time in the air.

Ten minutes wouldn't be enough.

"There's the camp," Dagoberto whispered to Encarnacion. "And there's the second machine gun nest. Now follow me. Use your machete if we run into anyone."

"I'll do my part," Encarnacion promised, hefting his sword-like weapon.

Dagoberto knew he would. He'd seen the villager work his savagery in the first machine gun nest, killing two of the rebels before they were even aware that anything was amiss. *Encarnacion lost his family to the rebels,* the *Cinchis* soldier reflected, creeping through the darkness. *Now he's getting his revenge.*

The squad leader turned to the villagers and soldiers encircling him in the darkness. "If any shooting starts," he whispered, "fire at the camp below. Remember, we're not going to hold any ground. Start retreating as soon as they charge. Then we'll drop back and wait for the helicopter to come. Only then will we fight to win."

He and Encarnacion then turned and made their way along the rough path leading to the second machine gun nest. The trail overlooked the valley where the rebel camp was located. All was quiet except for a cluster of men who sat near the entrance of the cave. The soldier could easily discern the cavern with his

NVGs, which turned the little light from inside its mouth into a bright glow.

Behind the soldier, Encarnacion stumbled, sending a small but noisy rock slide down the steep path. Both the villager and the *Cinchis* dropped to their hands and knees and remained motionless. Dagoberto held his breath, wondering if anyone had noticed the noise.

But the men in the camp continued their loud conversation.

The soldier glanced toward the machine gun nest, where he was satisfied to note that the guards had fallen asleep. *We're still safe,* he realized, rising to his feet.

The two continued up the path, finally reaching their destination. One of the rebels stirred as the soldier crept into the emplacement; the silenced Makarov pistol in Dagoberto's hand cracked twice and the rebel fell backward, clutching at his chest.

As the second rebel sprang to his feet with the muffled shot, Encarnacion swung his blade.

The insurgent crumpled to the sand, his head spilling into the dirt and rolling away from his body. Dagoberto glanced at the villager, who wore an odd smile as he wiped his blade clean on his victim's shirt.

"What's happening up there?" a voice inquired in Spanish, drifting up from the camp below. "Is everything all right?"

"Everything's fine," Dagoberto answered.

"Who is that?" the voice called.

"It's okay," Dagoberto yelled again, swiveling the machine gun around to cover the camp. He snapped off the safety, aimed, and opened fire on the rebels below. The *Cinchis* was rewarded with the sight of eight rebels dropping into the dust as the others, many of them just waking up, scurried for cover behind boulders.

For several minutes, as the soldier thought he had the insurgents at bay, he toyed with the idea that he might prevail without calling in the American chopper. Then a LAW-80 warhead came out of nowhere, exploding next to the machine gun nest and pelting Dagoberto and Encarnacion with stones. He observed another rocket flash and, within seconds, it detonated to his right.

He realized they were getting close and would probably score with a couple of more tries; it was time to initiate the retreat to draw the rebels from their hiding places. "Come on!" the *Cinchis* yelled to Encarnacion as the soldier leaped from the emplacement. The two ran toward the villagers, Dagoberto yelling, "Retreat! Retreat!" at the top of his voice to guarantee that the rebels would hear.

As bullets licked the stones around him, Dagoberto did not wait to see what the insurgents would do. A third LAW hit the machine gun emplacement that he and Encarnacion had just left, the concussion knocking him to his knees.

This is definitely a good time to leave, he thought, getting back to his feet and following the fleeing villagers. The important question was whether the rebels would follow.

His question was answered almost immediately as he and the others raced along the ridge. A heavy barrage rang down from the hill to their left.

"The rebels are flanking us!" one of the *Cinchis* yelled to Dagoberto.

The squad leader said nothing, struggling to remove the transmitter from his pocket. It was past time to radio the American chopper in.

Now we'll see if my idea will work, Oz thought after receiving the frantic call for help from Dagoberto. The fuel leak had stabilized only after the A tank had emptied itself. That left them only enough fuel in their second tank for slightly more than ten minutes in the air.

To conserve on fuel, Oz had set down on a nearby ridge and shut down the engines to wait for the radio message from the *Cinchis.* The pilot hoped this would buy them enough flight time to engage the rebels, land, rescue the hostages, and escape. He knew they didn't have enough fuel to reach Piton; they would have to go at least part of the way on foot.

Oz started the chopper's twin engines.

The machine sputtered, coughed, and came to life. Within seconds, Oz throttled the engines to their full power and connected the clutch to join the rotors to the engine; the rotor tachometer showed the blades attaining their full speed.

Oz lifted the fighting machine into the air.

"Almost everything looks good," Death Song said, checking the computer readout. "But the fuel's definitely going to be gone in nine more minutes."

"With a little luck, that should be enough time in the air," Oz replied, bleakly recalling the old chopper pilot joke about how hard it was to fly with your fingers crossed.

Within two minutes the MH-60K had leaped a foothill and was hurtling downward toward the rebels, who had the villagers pinned down on a ridge 500 meters east of the guerrilla camp.

The helicopter skimmed a granite outcropping, coming in low behind the rebels. Oz aligned the nose of the helicopter with the largest mass of men and tapped the rocket launch button on the control column with his little finger.

A 70mm rocket jumped from its pod, its engine bursting to life. With a blur of speed, it reached the men and exploded on the face of the rock, scattering rebels like rag dolls. The chopper traveled over the insurgents, machine gun pod and Miniguns blazing.

Oz banked and descended into another attack run, chasing the last nine guerrillas who were fleeing toward their camp, leaving their wounded comrades behind. He twisted the chopper in the air, concentrating his machine gun fire on the line and only releasing the fire button when the last of the men had fallen.

The *Cinchis* and villagers on the ground joined the chopper in a final deadly salvo. The chopper hurtled over the rebels, its Miniguns erupting behind Oz.

The pilot circled the battlefield, surveying the damage; all the insurgents appeared to be either dead or dying. "Kill the fuel emergency warning," he ordered Death Song. Oz already knew they'd nearly exhausted their fuel without the alarm haranguing him.

The warning beep stopped; the radio sputtered to life. "NS-1, this is Ground One," Dagoberto called. "It looks clear down here."

"I'm heading for the camp," Oz answered. "I'm

not going to pick you up because we're nearly out of fuel. Over.''

"We'll continue on foot and meet you there. I don't think there can be more than a few of the rebels in the camp, but I'm not positive."

"We'll find out in a couple of minutes," Oz radioed back. "See you there. Over and out."

Zurita dragged the woman into the cave. *Damn those Americans,* he raged. They'd managed to sucker his men into the open and—judging from the sound of the explosions and shooting—must surely have killed the majority of them in an ambush.

Reaching the rear of the cave, he stopped next to his other four prisoners and spoke to Yannera, the only man who'd stayed behind to help guard the prisoners. "Go outside and try to down the Yankee chopper when it approaches," he ordered.

"I'll do my best, comrade."

Zurita watched the young rebel leave, then turned toward the American geologist. "As for you, it's time to tell your secret. If you don't, you will have the pleasure of seeing me kill your woman here."

"You claim to be helping the Indians," Lloyd said, "and yet you're trying to rob them of their gold. But the imperialists you so despise are helping the Indians keep the gold."

"Shut up," Zurita said. "This isn't a schoolboy debate. You know the Peruvian government wouldn't do anything for your precious villagers if it couldn't get a big share of the gold." Zurita pulled Maria's hair, forcing her head back to expose her neck; then he drew his knife, looking the American in the eye. "Now tell me!"

"I'll tell you," Lloyd promised.

Zurita could hear the thumping of the helicopter blades. The rebel started to flee into the maze of tunnels at the end of the cave, then hesitated. *If I could learn where the gold is, my mission wouldn't be a total failure,* he thought. Hastening back toward the prisoners, the insurgent grasped Maria's hair, intending to drag her along with him. She moaned in pain and struggled, but was unable to get to her feet because of the tight ropes binding her hands and legs.

Zurita pushed his face into the American's. "Tell me or I start the slaughter," he threatened, his blade flashing toward Maria's throat.

The geologist leaped before the rebel could react, the severed ropes that had constrained his arms and legs dropping away. Lloyd's SOG knife cut into Zurita's neck, severing the revolutionary's jugular vein and the carotid arteries next to it with a single slash. The guerrilla struggled to fight back but his knife hand was clamped firmly in the American giant's fist.

Zurita released his hold on Maria's hair, snatching at the American's blade as it sliced toward him. He struggled to shout for Yannera as Lloyd's blade connected with a second savage cut, slashing his voice box to make him mute.

Blood gushed in spurts, the dark, red liquid spewing in a stream stretching almost five feet, bathing the geologist. The guerrilla's vision went black as his brain, starved for oxygen, closed off non-vital body functions. His nose filled with the smell of blood and, in a dying hallucination, he was transported to an ancient Incan ritual. Prisoners lined the ancient temple of his apparition, waiting to be sacrificed to the *Sapa Inca.*

And then all thought ceased in Zurita's oxygen-starved brain. Lloyd held the limp rebel until he was certain he was dead, then tossed the lifeless body into a dark corner of the cave.

The geologist was suddenly aware that Maria was sobbing.

He knelt to cut her bonds with his folding knife. "Shhh," he told her, hesitant to hold her in his blood-soaked arms. "It's almost over."

He quickly released the other wide-eyed prisoners.

The MH-60K's engines began to sputter as Oz whipped the chopper above the guerrilla camp, searching for any sign of remaining insurgents.

"Captain, there's a rebel with a rocket launcher," Death Song warned. "Behind the boulder at one o'clock."

"I see him," Oz said.

Yannera raised the launch tube.

The American pilot shoved the control column to starboard and lifted the collective pitch lever moments before the guerrilla launched his rocket. The chopper leaped the ridge and descended behind it. The rocket's backblast lit the sky behind the American chopper as Death Song released a flare.

The Redeye II rocket flashed over the ridge, homed in on the flare, and exploded behind the Americans.

The engines on the MH-60K failed.

Oz immediately lowered the collective pitch lever as the chopper automatically separated its rotors from the transmission, sending the helicopter into an autorotation mode that would slowly drop them safely to the earth. The pilot kicked a rudder pedal, which continued to function since the tail rotor was still driven by the main rotor. His action circled them back toward the camp as they descended.

"O.T.," Oz called over the intercom, "if I give you a clear shot, do you think you can take him with the Minigun? You'll only have time for one shot, and we'll have to be careful, since the hostages may be in the cave behind him."

"Let me take him with my carbine," the warrant officer suggested.

"Let's do it."

O.T. jerked his Colt Commando from the metal bracket that held it close to his chair and twisted the battery switch on the Aimpoint scope atop the rifle. Tentatively sighting through it from his open side window, he alerted the pilot: "I'm ready."

"You won't have long," Oz cautioned as they barely cleared the ridge and fell toward the rebel stronghold. The aircraft continued its autorotation descent, the pilot guiding it with the control column and rudders so it turned with its port side facing the mouth of the cave, flying almost silently without its engines.

As the chopper dropped serenely toward the ground, a startled Yannera lifted another Redeye to his shoulder, activated the weapon, and sighted through its scope.

"Now!" Oz yelled.

Before the rebel could lock onto his target, a single shot left the MH-60K.

Yannera collapsed silently to the dirt, a .22-caliber bullet hole between his eyes.

The helicopter settled onto the ground at the same moment Lloyd and the other hostages appeared at the mouth of the cave. "Luger and O.T., let's prepare to destroy the chopper to prevent compromise. Then we'll get out of here before what's left of the rebels start straggling in."

"Will do, captain."

Minutes later, after contacting Warner to apprise him of the situation, the helicopter crew helped the hostages climb toward the ridge where they joined the *Cinchis* and other villagers for the long trek back to Piton.

"Three hundred yards and my feet are already sore," Luger complained.

"Too much soft living," O.T. suggested.

There was a massive explosion as the abandoned MH-60K's ordnance detonated in the valley behind them. Three seconds later, the second timed explosive set off the cache of dynamite the rebels had stored in the tunnel. As the flames leaped into the sky, bathing everyone in light, Oz was startled to see how blood-soaked Lloyd was.

"Are you injured?" the pilot asked.

"No. This is someone else's blood," Lloyd answered.

"I'd hate to see the other guy," O.T. quipped, only half in jest.

"So what took you guys so long?" the geologist teased, turning away from the dying flames to trudge up the ridge, hand in hand with Maria.

E P I L O G U E

"Did you guys enjoy your nice, relaxing visit to Peru?" Bishop asked Oz over the intercom seconds before their new chopper lifted off the courtyard of the Peruvian government palace.

"A nice, restful vacation," the pilot answered, bringing the MH-60K onto its new course heading. "But a guy can only take so much boredom."

"Yeah," Bishop answered, "I know *exactly* what you mean."

The pilot steered the aircraft over the three-story alabaster palace elaborately embellished in the style of sixteenth-century Spanish architecture. The crimson-and-white state flag flapped in the wind as armed guards in elegant dress uniforms and chromed helmets paced along the high, wrought-iron fence surrounding the courtyard.

The other MH-60K and the three Apache gunships escorting the vice-president fell into formation behind Oz's chopper. The five American aircraft were headed for the Peruvian air base, where a U.S. C-5A Galaxy waited to transport them back to the states.

Oz thought of Piton for a moment and wondered

again whether the newly discovered treasure would prove to be a blessing for the villagers or a curse. Nearly an eighth of the inhabitants of the village were injured or dead; almost a fourth were homeless. Plus, Piton would always be a target for the Shining Path.

Weighing against these negatives were the plans Ramero and Lloyd had for the hamlet: a new school, a doctor, better housing. If all went well, the villagers would step into the modern age, and their children would have the skills and opportunities to find jobs almost anywhere in the world.

Are they really any worse off than the rest of us? he asked himself. Only time would tell.

As the helicopters flashed through the morning sunlight, leaving Lima far behind, Oz's thoughts turned homeward. *It will be nice to get back to the states.* A familiar house; a pillow that fit his head. . . .

In just a few hours, they'd be home.

Duncan Long is internationally recognized as a firearms expert, and has had over twenty books published on that subject, as well as numerous magazine articles. In addition to his nonfiction writing, Long has written a science fiction novel, *Antigrav Unlimited.* He has an MA in music composition, and has worked as a rock musician; he has spent nine years teaching in public schools. Duncan Long lives in eastern Kansas with his wife and two children.